FOREVER AND ALWAYS SERIES - BOOK 3

A SISTER'S Secret

NORA BLOOM

Chapter One

The golden glow of the setting sun spilled through the sheer curtains, casting a warm hue across the living room where laughter bubbled like a brook in springtime. Daniel was seated cross-legged on the floor, constructing an intricate fortress from wooden blocks, his brow furrowed in concentration. With her curly brown hair bouncing with each giggle, Abigail maneuvered her doll to be the fortress's queen, commanding it with a high-pitched voice that was all authority and mirth. Ethan had joined in, too, even though he felt he was too old to play anymore. Being with his younger siblings often persuaded him to reconnect with his inner child anyway—for their sake, of course. Because they always begged him to join them. And cradled in Lisa's arms, little Julia cooed softly, her tiny fingers wrapped around one of Lisa's, anchoring herself to the heart of the family.

Lisa glanced up from Julia to find Oliver watching

them, his blue eyes tender and soft around the edges, as if the scene before him were a painting he wished to preserve forever. He knelt beside Daniel, who had just turned six, offering a block to fortify the ramparts and winking at Lisa over his son's head. It was a simple gesture, yet it spoke volumes of the love and solidarity that had become the foundation of their blended family.

"Smells like dinner's ready," Oliver murmured, his voice low and resonant. The scent of freshly baked bread wafted through the house, a testament to the hours spent in the kitchen, hands dusted with flour, shoulders brushing, as they prepared their meal together.

"Come on, kiddos, let's wash up!" Lisa announced, her tone infused with the anticipation of the feast awaiting them.

Daniel reluctantly abandoned his fortress while Abigail scooped up her doll, declaring that royalty must dine as well. Together, they scampered toward the bathroom, their footsteps light and carefree.

In the dining room, the table was set with mismatched plates and cutlery that told stories of past lives and new beginnings. Each chair was pulled out, waiting to be filled with the warmth of familial love. As they gathered, Ethan took it upon himself to help Julia into her high chair, his protective instincts always at the forefront despite his tender age. The baby's legs protested being restrained since she just learned to walk.

They sat, hand in hand, forming an unbroken circle around the table laden with dishes that steamed with promise.

"Can I say grace?" Abigail asked, her small voice earnest in the quiet that had settled over them.

"Of course, sweetheart," Lisa said, squeezing Oliver's hand—a silent thank you for the peace they'd found in each other.

Abigail's words were a simple expression of gratitude for the food, their safety, and, most of all, for being together. As they echoed "Amen" in unison, a sense of fulfillment swept through Lisa, a thrilling rush from knowing they had weathered storms to reach this harbor of joy. The golden crust of the homemade bread broke with a satisfying crunch under Lisa's knife, releasing a yeasty cloud that mingled with the aroma of roasted vegetables and seasoned chicken.

"Let's eat!" Oliver declared, and the spell was broken, replaced by the clatter of serving spoons and the chatter of children eager to share the events of their day.

As they passed dishes and poured drinks, laughter again filled the room, weaving a tapestry of contentment that hung tangibly in the air. Lisa caught Oliver's gaze and held it, a silent conversation passing between them—one of resilience, shared dreams, and the unspoken thrill of navigating life's journey together.

Lisa's hands moved with practiced ease, dusted lightly with flour as she slid a batch of cinnamon swirl scones into the oven. The warmth from the open flame brushed against her cheeks, a comforting reminder of the many mornings spent perfecting recipes that now tempted the townsfolk into their cozy establishment. Oliver, his sleeves rolled up to his elbows, was at the other end of the café, meticulously sanding the edges of a cedar coffee table he had been working on for weeks. The rhythmic sound of the sandpaper against the wood was a soothing backdrop to the murmur of customers.

"Morning, Lisa!" Mrs. Dalton called out, stepping inside with the bell above the door chiming her arrival. "I swear, the whole town can smell your baking today!"

"Good morning, Marjorie," Lisa replied, her voice laced with pride. "I hope it tastes as good as it smells."

"It always does, dear," Mrs. Dalton said, her eyes twinkling as she eyed the display case.

Around them, the café hummed with life. Locals sat in mismatched chairs at tables Oliver had lovingly restored, each telling its own story. The air was alive with the clink of coffee cups and the soft laughter of patrons who came not only for the food and furniture but for the atmosphere that Lisa and Oliver had cultivated—a blend of rustic charm and heartfelt hospitality.

"Oliver, this piece is stunning," Mr. Jenkins, the local librarian, remarked, running a hand over the smooth grain of the table. "You've truly outdone yourself."

"Thanks, Sam," Oliver responded, his eyes lighting up with the compliment. He looked across the room at Lisa, sharing a smile that spoke volumes. They were more than business partners; they were artisans of their own future, building it with every cake baked and every piece of wood shaped.

As the morning gave way to afternoon, the ebb and flow of customers remained steady. Tourists, drawn by word-of-mouth recommendations, snapped photos of the woodwork and savored the homemade pastries. Lisa noticed how they lingered, soaking in the ambiance, reluctant to leave the little oasis she and Oliver had created.

"Seems like we're becoming quite the spot on the map," Oliver whispered to Lisa in a rare quiet moment during the lunchtime rush.

"Only because you make this place impossible to forget," she replied, squeezing his hand.

Their connection was palpable, not just to each other but to everyone who crossed the threshold. It was as if the shop throbbed with their shared pulse—a beacon of dedication and love in the heart of a small town that had become their biggest supporter.

As the sun began its descent, casting golden hues through the front windows, Lisa caught sight of the community board brimming with flyers for events and services. Their upcoming woodworking class was already filled with sign-ups, a testament to the trust and respect they'd garnered.

"Look at this, Ollie," she said, pointing at the board. "We might need to schedule another class."

"Or two," he chuckled, the lines around his eyes crinkling with delight. The thought of teaching others their craft and passing on a piece of themselves was both thrilling and a touch daunting. Oliver never liked being in front of a crowd much, but it was easier with Lisa by his side.

The day wound down with the last customer leaving with a satisfied sigh and a promise to return. As Lisa turned the sign to "Closed," she leaned back against the door, capturing the scene before her—the tables filled with traces of joy, the lingering scent of coffee, and Oliver locking away his tools, his hands still bearing the evidence of hard work.

"Another day," she murmured, contentment sweeping over her.

"Another day living our dreams," Oliver agreed, crossing the room to wrap his arms around her. In this space they had carved out for themselves, amidst the sawdust and sugar, they found their haven, wrapped up in the heartwarming embrace of a community that had become their family.

The sun dipped low on the horizon, painting the town square in hues of orange and pink as Lisa and Oliver stepped into the thrum of the annual Harvest Festival. Children dashed by with painted faces and balloons while a local band filled the air with lively tunes that beckoned even the shyest toes to tap.

"Isn't this something?" Lisa beamed, her eyes reflecting the festival lights strung from lamppost to lamppost like stars brought down to earth. She felt Oliver's hand tighten around hers, an unspoken acknowledgment of their shared joy.

"Hey, there's the dynamic duo!" Mayor Johnson called out, his voice booming above the chatter as he approached them with open arms. Murmurs of affection and admiration followed their path, the couple weaving through claps on the back and warm embraces. It was clear they were more than just business owners; they were becoming the heart of the community.

"Care for a dance, milady?" Oliver teased, bowing slightly. The playful glint in his eyes revealed a side of him that flourished in these moments of carefree celebration.

Lisa laughed, the sound mingling with the music, and accepted. They swayed together amidst fellow townsfolk, sharing smiles and laughter, their movements a silent language of love. It was here, among friends and neighbors, where the thrill of belonging wrapped around them like a cherished quilt.

As the evening waned and the last song played, they reluctantly bid farewell to the festivities, promising to carry the warmth of the town's embrace back home.

The following morning, the family found themselves at the cusp of the ocean, the beach sprawling before them like an untouched canvas. Ethan, Abigail, and Daniel bolted toward the shoreline, their squeals dissolving into the rhythmic crash of waves, with Julia struggling to keep up.

"Race you to the water!" Ethan challenged, his voice hitching with excitement.

"Last one in is a rotten jellyfish!" Daniel shouted, not far behind.

"Remember to stay where we can see you!" Lisa called after them as they jumped into the cold water, squealing, but her words were swept away by the wind. She felt a chill as the breeze hit her and thought the kids had to be crazy to go in the water in September when it was only fifty degrees out. She watched as Oliver helped Abigail hoist a kite into the sky, his silhouette framed against the backdrop of endless blue, a contented sigh escaping her lips.

"Look at them," Oliver said, returning to Lisa's side, his gaze lingering on the children who were now out of the water again, building a sandcastle fortress. "This—this right here—is what life's all about."

Lisa nodded, the breeze catching strands of her wavy brown hair. She clasped Oliver's hand, feeling the grains of sand stick to her skin, a tactile reminder of the simple pleasures surrounding them.

"Let's build our own castle," she suggested, the

spark of challenge in her eyes igniting a similar flame in his.

Together, they set to work, crafting turrets and walls, their creation growing more elaborate by the minute, their laughter joining the chorus of their children's. The suspense of each wave threatening to wash away their efforts only added to the thrill, a metaphor for the life they had built—beautiful, fragile, yet resilient.

As the day gave way to the soft glow of dusk and the kites were reeled in, they stood back to admire their sandy empire, knowing the sea would soon reclaim it. But the memories, the pure, undeniable happiness etched into this moment, would remain theirs forever.

The beach trip concluded with the family gathered at the water's edge, watching the sun sink beneath the waves. Lisa leaned into Oliver, her heart brimming with gratitude.

The hum of the cafe's espresso machine fell silent, and in that quiet, Lisa caught Oliver's eye from across the room. His hands were still, resting atop a half-finished wooden sculpture that was meant to be their next big seller. The ledger was open on the counter before her, screaming a truth they both had tried to avoid: numbers still in red, margins too thin. The café was doing better than ever, but the numbers still weren't as good as they needed them to be.

"Ollie," she called softly, not wanting to worry the children who were upstairs preparing for their school play.

Oliver set down his chisel and came to her, the scent of sawdust and coffee mingling between them. "I know," he said, his voice steady despite the storm brewing in his eyes. "I've seen the books."

Lisa bit her lip, her gaze drifting back to the page. "We could... maybe cut back on some supplies—hold off on the new espresso machine?"

He nodded, wrapping an arm around her waist and pulling her close as if to physically shield her from the weight of their worries. "And I can try to sell some pieces online—expand our reach beyond the town?"

Their foreheads touched in a silent exchange of strength. "We'll make it work together," Lisa murmured, feeling the knot in her chest loosen just a little at the promise in Oliver's eyes.

"Like we always do," he replied, a half-smile breaking through.

"Mom! Oliver!" Ethan's voice echoed as he bounded down the stairs, Abigail and Daniel trailing behind him. All three were adorned in costumes vibrant with color and childish enthusiasm. Julia stumbled behind them, trying to keep up with their longer legs.

"Look at you!" Lisa exclaimed, the financial crisis momentarily forgotten.

"Is it time?" Oliver asked, glancing at his watch.

"Twenty minutes until curtain!" Ethan announced proudly, puffing out his chest.

They hurried to the school auditorium, where parents and neighbors filled the seats, buzzing with anticipation. As the lights dimmed, Lisa squeezed Oliver's hand, her heart swelling with pride.

The curtains lifted, and there they were: Ethan as the brave knight, Abigail as the clever wizard, and little Daniel, the enchanted forest creature. Their lines were delivered with adorable determination, their movements exaggerated yet endearing. The play unfolded, a whirlwind of magic and triumph, and Lisa felt her throat tighten at the sight of their children so boldly claiming their moment.

When the final bow was taken, the applause was thunderous. Lisa and Oliver were on their feet, clapping until their hands ached, whistles and cheers escaping their lips.

"Did you see Daniel's somersault?" Oliver leaned in, his voice thick with pride.

"And Abby's spell-casting? She's a natural!" Lisa beamed.

Ethan caught sight of them from the stage, his grin wide and victorious. They met backstage, enveloped in the chaos of excited children and proud parents, yet their family felt like the only people in the world.

"Did I do good?" Daniel's eyes sparkled up at Lisa.

"You were amazing, sweetheart," she said, lifting him into a hug that spoke volumes of love and reassurance. She wasn't his biological mother, but he felt closer to her with every day that passed.

"Best night ever!" Abigail declared, bouncing on the balls of her feet.

"Let's celebrate," Oliver suggested, and the idea was met with ecstatic nods.

"I have hot chocolate and cinnamon buns ready at the café," Lisa said.

As they left the auditorium, Lisa glanced at the stars beginning to pepper the night sky. Challenges would come and go, but these moments—these victories both on stage and within the walls of their home—were the true measure of their lives. Together, they walked toward the café, the children chattering excitedly, their future as bright as the constellations above.

Chapter Two

The door to the Seabreeze Café swung open with a purpose that matched the brisk Alaskan morning breeze, causing the chime above to sing its metallic greeting. Heads turned almost in unison toward the entrance as Sheriff James "Jim" Coleman stepped inside. The hum of conversation dwindled into a suspenseful silence, punctuated only by the gentle clinking of coffee cups being set down mid-sip and the soft scrape of chair legs against the wooden floor.

Oliver Thompson, his hands steady from years of coaxing shapes out of wood, felt a tremor run through them as he caught sight of the sheriff. The man's silhouette was all too familiar—a harbinger of order and, occasionally, bearer of bad tidings in their close-knit community. Oliver's pulse thudded at his temples, his heart drumming a rhythm that spoke of both anticipation and dread.

The cafe's cozy warmth did little to ease the sudden

chill that seemed to coil around Oliver's spine. He stood frozen behind the counter, his fingers tightening involuntarily around the handle of the coffee pot he'd been about to refill. His blue eyes, usually warm with laughter shared with his woodworking students or love for his family, now mirrored the stormy gray of the sea during a squall.

Sheriff Coleman's boots echoed on the hardwood floor, a staccato beat that commanded attention and respect. As he navigated through the maze of tables, the locals watched, their expressions a blend of curiosity and concern. They knew, just as Oliver did, that the sheriff's presence here was no social call. It was as if the room itself held its breath, bracing for the unknown.

Oliver's grip on the coffee pot slackened, and he placed it back onto the warmer with a care that belied the turmoil brewing within him. He swallowed hard, trying to dislodge the knot that had formed in his throat. Each step the sheriff took toward him felt like a countdown, a tick-tock toward a revelation he wasn't sure he was ready to face.

"Morning, Sheriff," Oliver managed to say, his voice betraying none of the unease that swarmed like bees in his stomach. The forced smile he offered was one he had mastered over the years—a mask to hide the scars left by a family history that always seemed to loom over him like a shadow.

Sheriff Coleman nodded in acknowledgment; his stern expression softened ever so slightly by the lines of genuine concern etched around his eyes. The air was thick with unspoken words, and the café, once abuzz with the day's gossip and laughter, was now a silent witness to the palpable tension that enveloped both men.

The sheriff's boots thudded against the faded linoleum floor, a steady drum that matched the racing of Oliver's heart. He watched the man weave through the scattered chairs and tables, his towering frame cutting a path straight to the counter where Oliver stood, trapped by expectation and dread.

"Oliver," Sheriff Coleman's voice was low, the timbre barely rising above the hum of the refrigerators in the corner. "We need to talk. Privately."

Every pair of eyes in the café seemed to burn into Oliver's back, igniting the anxiety that simmered beneath his skin. His hands gripped the edge of the counter until his knuckles blanched. There was no mistaking the seriousness etched into the lines of the sheriff's face, no escaping the urgency that laced his words.

"Of course, Sheriff," Oliver replied, his tone steadier than he felt. With a glance at the curious onlookers, he wiped his palms on his apron and rounded the counter. The familiar weight of responsibility, a constant companion since his youth, settled heavily on his shoulders as he followed the sheriff's lead.

They moved together through the narrow hallway that ran like an artery behind the cafe's public facade. Each step reverberated off the tight walls, a solemn echo to their silent procession.

Oliver felt the space around him shrink, compressing the air until it became something thick and tangible.

The small office at the end of the hall was a cramped room cluttered with old filing cabinets and stacks of paperwork.

Sheriff Coleman stepped inside first, his presence dominating the confined space. Oliver entered hesitantly, the door clicking shut behind him with an ominous finality. Alone now, cut off from the outside world, the two men faced each other—each braced for the impact of words yet unspoken, each aware that whatever came next would irrevocably alter the course of the day.

Sheriff Coleman's hand reached up, pausing momentarily before grasping the brim of his hat. He pulled it off slowly, revealing a furrowed brow and a scalp dusted with gray. The air seemed to still in that cramped office as if it, too, anticipated the weight of what was to come.

"Oliver," he began, his voice uncharacteristically gentle yet laden with an unmistakable sorrow. "I'm afraid I've got some bad news about your sister, Michelle."

The words hung there, suspended in the stale office air. Oliver's heart, already pounding against the walls of his chest, threatened to break free.

"My sister?" His voice sounded foreign to him, distant and hollow. "What about her?"

"It's... she's passed away, Oliver." The sheriff's eyes, usually so steady, flickered with emotion. "I am so very sorry."

A cold tide of shock washed over Oliver's senses, dousing the embers of hope that always burned for reconciliation, for another chance to see Michelle and mend the fractures of the past. His sister was a part of his life that had been absent yet omnipresent like the shadow of a dream long forgotten upon waking.

"Passed away?" Oliver echoed, his mind recoiling, seeking refuge in denial. How could it be? Michelle, with her rebellious spirit and wild laughter, was gone? She was out there somewhere, or so he had always believed, living her life.

Memories surged through him, unbidden. Images of a young girl with braided hair, her face alight with mischief as they played along the rugged coastline. He had been a protector from childhood's squabbles and scraped knees. And then, the years peeled away to reveal darker times when their paths diverged into forests thick with silence and unspoken regrets.

"Oliver?" The sheriff's hand rested on his shoulder, grounding him to the present.

"Wh-what happened?" Oliver's words stumbled out, tripping over themselves as his thoughts raced. She had been gone so long, a whisper of a life that once ran parallel to his own. What had claimed her? Was it the wilderness she sought or something more sinister?

"Details are scarce right now," Sheriff Coleman admitted. "But I promise you, we will find out. We owe it to her... to you."

Oliver nodded, numbness seeping into his limbs. A lifetime of questions bloomed in his chest, thorny and wild. Yet amidst the tumult of grief and confusion, one thing stood clear and unwavering: he would unearth the truth of his sister's fate, for the love that persisted through absence and silence, for the bond not even death could sever.

Lisa paused, the clink of coffee cups and murmurs from the café fading into a distant hum as she caught sight of Sheriff Coleman leaving the office and finding a seat at a nearby table. He caught Lisa's eye, and his expression seemed to give her permission to go to Oliver. The subtle furrow of her brow spoke volumes of her intuition that something was amiss. A mother's instinct, woven with threads of past adversities, honed her sensitivity to the unseen troubles lurking beneath the surface of everyday life. She wiped her hands on her apron, the fabric a testament to countless hours of nurturing and care within these walls, and moved with purpose toward the narrow hallway leading to the back office.

The door was ajar, revealing Oliver standing still as a statue, his usually warm eyes now pools of despair. Lisa's heart contracted at the sight, a silent alarm ringing through her veins. Without hesitation, she crossed the threshold, her footsteps soft but swift. As if guided by a force greater than herself, she reached Oliver's side in an instant, her arms enfolding him with a strength forged from years of facing her own demons and emerging resilient.

"Oliver?" Her voice was gentle yet laced with concern as she held him close, feeling the tremors that shook his frame.

His voice was fractured by emotion, barely louder than a whisper. "It's Michelle... she's gone, Lisa."

The words hung between them, each syllable laden with a heartbreaking finality. Lisa's embrace tightened as she absorbed the blow of his grief, the sharp edge of loss cutting through the air.

Tears blurred her vision, empathy blooming within her like a delicate yet persistent flower pushing through winter's frost.

"Oh, Oliver, I'm so sorry," she managed to say, her voice thick with sorrow. Her hazel eyes, always so attentive and kind, now reflected the shared pain that connected their souls in this moment of raw vulnerability.

In the quiet of the office, with only the faint sounds of life continuing outside, they stood entwined by more than just their arms. Heavy with the loss of a sister he had both adored and mourned for years, Oliver's heart found a glimmer of solace in Lisa's unwavering support. And as the reality of his loss seeped into the depths of their being, they leaned on one another, finding a semblance of peace amidst the turmoil.

Sheriff Coleman's silhouette loomed in the doorway, his presence a solemn anchor in the storm of emotion that raged through the small office. The lines etching his face seemed to deepen as he took in the sight of Oliver and Lisa, their bodies interlocked in a desperate bid for comfort.

"I'm sorry to be the bearer of such news," he said, his voice a low rumble of empathy that resonated in the confined space. "Oliver, Lisa, I want you both to know that I'll turn over every stone to give you answers. We owe Michelle that much. We all loved her."

The sheriff's eyes, usually so sharp and assessing, now held a softness that belied his gruff exterior. It was clear that beneath the badge and the years of upholding law and order, Jim Coleman's heart bled just as theirs did.

Oliver nodded, his jaw clenched in an effort to stave off the swell of emotions threatening to spill forth once more. Lisa, feeling the tension in her husband's frame, drew him closer, her own grief mingling with his as they sought refuge in each other's arms.

"Thank you, Jim," Oliver managed to say, his words muffled against Lisa's hair. The café around them faded into irrelevance, the clinking of dishes and murmur of patrons nothing but a distant echo against the gravity of their loss.

Lisa's tears were silent. Her strength at this moment manifested not through stoicism but through the tenderness with which she held Oliver.

Together, they stood, wrapped in a cocoon of shared sorrow and love. The world outside might continue its relentless march forward, but within the confines of the office, time seemed to pause, allowing them just a moment to breathe—to absorb the shock of a universe abruptly and irrevocably altered.

In the quiet aftermath of the sheriff's promise, the air buzzed with unspoken questions and fears about what lay ahead.

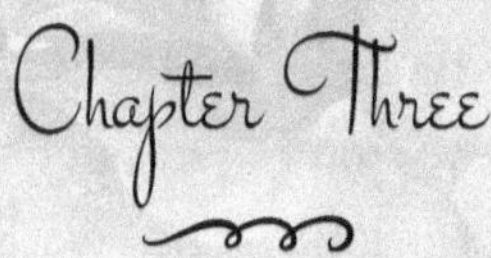

Chapter Three

The edges of the worn wooden table bit into Oliver's fingers as his grip tightened, a futile attempt to anchor himself against the news that had just capsized his world. The sheriff's words still echoed in the room, bouncing off walls hung with pictures of happier times, now tainted with the grief of loss.

Oliver nodded silently to Sheriff Coleman, his throat too tight to form words. He could feel the shock painted across his face, a mirror of the heartbreak he saw in Lisa's eyes.

"We should go," he finally managed. His voice was a stranger's—a hollow sound that seemed inadequate amidst the swirling emotions threatening to overwhelm him.

"Your parents are expecting us," Sheriff Coleman added gently, his stern features softened with empathy.

As they drove through town, the familiar sights blurred past Oliver and Lisa, leaving them wrapped in an oppressive silence broken only by the occasional gravel crunch beneath the tires. The sheriff's cruiser rolled to a stop outside the Thompson family home, secluded amongst the evergreens on the outskirts of their small town.

"I'll wait for you here," the sheriff said. "Give you some privacy to talk. I'll take you both home after. I already spoke with them earlier."

"Thanks, Jim," Oliver said.

"It's the least I can do. We all loved Michelle around here. She was a wild one, but we love those too."

Oliver stepped out into the biting air, its chill a stark contrast to the warmth he once felt here. His parents, John and Molly, stood waiting on the porch, their faces etched with sorrow and age, arms around each other in a rare display of unity. For a moment, it seemed as if the years of tension and unspoken regrets could be set aside, forgotten in the shadow of a shared tragedy.

"Mom, Dad," Oliver said, his voice cracking like thin ice beneath his feet.

"Oliver," Molly whispered, reaching out a hand that trembled as much from emotion as from the cold. Her gaze shifted to Lisa, offering a silent plea for understanding in these moments where words would always fall short.

They moved together, a family, broken and reassembling in the face of loss, each touch and glance a fragile thread weaving them closer. The creak of the porch underfoot punctuated their silent communion, a reminder of the many summers spent in laughter and the winters that left them isolated from one another.

As they crossed the threshold into the house, memories flooded back for Oliver—of Michelle's laughter echoing down the hallways, of arguments that left scars no winter could erase. In this space filled with both love and regret, the weight of the past pressed down upon them all, urging them to confront the secrets that had long cast shadows over their lives.

The heavy oak door closed behind them with a definitive thud, sealing Oliver, Lisa, and his parents in the living room that felt more like a mausoleum of past emotions than a place of comfort. Oliver's father, John, stood stiffly by the fireplace, his eyes flicking everywhere but at his son. Molly's hands were clasped tightly in her lap, her knuckles white with the effort as she stared at Oliver, her face a roadmap of sorrow etched deep into her skin.

"Oliver," John's voice was barely audible, a low rumble that didn't dare rise above a whisper, as if he feared what might come out if he allowed himself to speak any louder.

"Dad," Oliver replied, his own voice laden with years of words unsaid. The air crackled with tension, each breath they took seeming to stir up dust and memories best left undisturbed.

Standing beside Oliver, Lisa felt the tangible ache of the space between father and son. She reached out, her fingers brushing against Oliver's hand, which trembled ever so slightly. He looked down at their entwined hands, and his resolve seemed to waver for a moment. But then he squeezed back, a silent message of gratitude for her presence.

Molly finally broke the silence, standing with an effort that seemed to take everything out of her.

"I made some tea," she said, her voice cracking like the thin ice on the town's lake in early winter.

"Thank you," Lisa murmured, even as she felt the hollowness of the gesture. Tea couldn't mend the fractures in this family or warm the chill that had settled in the room.

They sat around a coffee table laden with mismatched cups and a teapot that had seen better days. Oliver's gaze lifted to meet his mother's, searching for something—anything—that might bridge the gap time had carved between them. But when Molly's eyes met his, all he found was a well of sadness so profound it threatened to pull him under.

"Michelle..." Oliver started, his voice breaking on his sister's name. The word hung in the air, a specter none of them could escape.

"Oliver," Molly whispered, reaching across the table, her fingers hesitating just shy of his arm. "We...."

"Mom, it's okay," he interrupted, unsure if he was comforting her or himself.

Lisa watched the man she loved grappling with his

pain; his shoulders were squared against the deluge of grief threatening to break through his carefully constructed dam. She felt the rawness of his soul laid bare, the boy who had lost his sister and now faced the ghosts of that loss head-on.

As they sipped their tea, each mouthful tasted of unspoken apologies and regrets. In the heart-wrenching silence that followed, the ticking of the clock on the mantel became a metronome to their collective heart-beat—a family united in sorrow, facing the remnants of a storm that had never truly passed.

Molly's fingers were interlinked tightly in her lap, her knuckles whitened with the strain. John cleared his throat, a deep, rumbling sound that seemed to echo off the walls of the dimly lit living room.

"Oliver, there's not a day that goes by that we don't think about what happened to Michelle," John began, his voice thick with emotion. The timbre of regret in his voice was raw and palpable. "We had our disagree-ments, God knows, but we never imagined...."

"Your father and I," Molly interjected, her eyes brimming with unshed tears, "we thought she'd come back once things cooled down. We were so angry at the time, too proud to go after her." She looked up, her gaze meeting Oliver's. "We failed her as parents."

Oliver's chest tightened as he listened to the tremble in his mother's words and watched his father struggle to maintain composure. Their confessions were like shards of glass, each one piercing deeper into his heart. The shadows of the past seemed to cling to the edges of the room, whispering of missed opportunities and fractured relationships.

"Arguments happen in every family," Oliver said, his voice steady despite the whirlwind of emotions inside him. "But this... this silence for ten years. It's more than just pride, isn't it? She left and never even called any of us and never told us why."

Molly's lips parted, but no sound emerged. She glanced at John, seeking solace in his presence, but found none. They were united in their grief yet isolated by their own guilt.

"Son," John started, but Oliver cut him off with a raised hand. "We need to let it go. There's no use in ripping up the past; we can't...."

"No, Dad. No more excuses, no more secrets, and no more lies. I need to know what really happened to Michelle."

He stood abruptly, feeling a surge of adrenaline coursing through his veins. His chair scraped loudly against the wooden floor, an abrupt declaration of his intent.

"Oliver," Lisa said, reaching out to touch his arm, her expression filled with admiration and concern.

He turned to her, his blue eyes blazing with a fierce determination that belied the gentle nature she knew so well. "I'm not getting any answers here, Lisa. They'll never tell me the truth. I need to find it myself. For Michelle."

"Then we'll do it together," she replied, her voice steady, though he could see the worry tugging at the corners of her smile.

Oliver nodded, grateful beyond words for her unwavering support. He faced his parents once more, his posture speaking of a man who would not be swayed from his course.

"Whatever it takes, I'm going to uncover the truth. Michelle deserves that much. We all do."

Outside, the sun dipped below the horizon, casting long shadows across the Thompsons' secluded home. Inside, as the last light of day faded, a new resolve took hold, propelling Oliver into the depths of a mystery that had lingered over their lives for far too long.

Gently closing the door behind them, Oliver and Lisa stepped out into the cooling twilight, their arms instinctively wrapping around each other. The world seemed eerily silent, save for the rustling of leaves in the breeze —a stark contrast to the heavy revelations that still echoed in their minds.

"God, I can't believe she's gone..." Oliver's voice trailed off as he clutched Lisa closer.

Lisa nestled her head against his chest, her presence a balm to the ache that had settled in his heart.

"We'll get through this," she murmured, her words muffled by his jacket.

As they reached the gravel driveway, pebbles crunching beneath their feet, Oliver stopped, looking back at the house that loomed in the fading light. It was as if the structure itself was burdened with untold stories, its windows reflecting not just the dying day but the ghosts of a past long hidden.

"Where do we even start?" Lisa asked with her gaze following his. Her hazel eyes, usually so warm, were now clouded with the weight of uncertainty.

"First, we need to find out where Michelle went after she left here." Oliver's hands were fists at his sides, the woodworker's callouses a testament to his ability to shape and fix things. But this wasn't wood; this was his life, and it would take more than skilled hands to put these pieces back together.

"Maybe someone in town knows something," Lisa suggested, her resilience shining despite the shadow of doubt. "Old friends, neighbors... there has to be someone who knows where she went."

"We could check social media, online records..." he trailed off, his mind racing with possibilities. There was a decade to cover in which Michelle could have built an entirely new life or met an untimely fate. They had searched for her back then but came up with nothing. He had never wanted to stop, but his parents had told him to let it go. He never should have listened to them.

"Let's start with what we know and go from there," Lisa said, her practicality grounding him as always. She pulled out her phone, tapping away to take notes. "We'll make a list tonight—people to talk to, places to visit, anything and everything that might lead us to her untold story."

Oliver gave a determined nod, feeling the stirrings of hope amidst the turmoil. "Whatever it takes."

They reached the police cruiser with Sheriff Coleman sitting in it, waiting for them. As Oliver opened the door for Lisa, he paused, allowing himself a moment to look into her eyes.

"Thank you," he whispered, the words thick with gratitude and love. "For being my partner in every sense."

"Always," she replied, squeezing his hand before sliding into the seat.

With one last glance at the darkened house, Oliver got into the car in the front seat next to the sheriff.

"You okay?" Sheriff Coleman asked.

Oliver nodded. "As okay as can be expected, I guess."

"It will get better," he said as the engine came to life with a soft purr.

***

"Oliver?" Lisa's voice broke through his reverie, laced with concern, as they stepped out of the cruiser and said goodbye and thank you to the sheriff.

"I know you said you were okay to the sheriff, but *are* you okay?"

He nodded, but his jaw clenched involuntarily. An urgency bubbled up inside him, the need for answers more pressing than ever.

Lisa reached out, her hand warm against his arm. "We'll find the truth, Ollie. But we can't let it consume us."

"I need to know, Lisa." His words were fervent, an undercurrent of desperation threading through them. He shot her a look that bore the intensity of his resolve. "I need to understand why she vanished—why she didn't come back."

Her eyes softened, though worry creased her brow. "Just... don't lose yourself in this search," Lisa murmured, her fingers tracing patterns over his knuckles. The fierce determination in his gaze unsettled her; she knew the peril in obsession's grip all too well.

He nodded, though his heart raced with impatience. There was no turning back, not when the shadows of the past clung so tenaciously. "I won't," he promised, more to himself than to her. But the promise felt hollow against the magnitude of what lay ahead.

With a deep breath, Oliver turned his attention to the café in front of him, both their home and workplace. Somehow, it looked different now. A few hours ago, saving this place and making it work had been the most important task in his life. But now, everything had changed. It was no longer his number one priority. He had gained a new mission in life and was bracing his heart for whatever truths lay hidden in the darkness ahead.

Chapter Four

Oliver Thompson's hands were worn and steady, the product of years of shaping wood into art. But that steadiness betrayed him as his phone began vibrating against the workshop's scarred oak table. The call's ID flashed "Sheriff Jim Coleman" on the screen, sending an involuntary shiver down Oliver's spine, a premonition that this was not a social call.

"Oliver," came the sheriff's voice, uncharacteristically shaky. "It's about your sister."

Something in the way the words hung heavily in the air caused Oliver's grip on the phone to tighten, his knuckles whitening as if trying to squeeze out a different reality from the one he feared was about to unfold. It had been a week since the news had hit him, and his sister's death had become all-consuming in his life.

"Jim?" Oliver asked, a palpable dread settling over him.

There was a pause—a silence too weighty for mere words—before the sheriff replied, "The autopsy is in, Oliver. She took her own life. I'm so sorry."

The world seemed to tilt on its axis, a surreal dissonance throwing every sense into chaos as the news clawed its way into Oliver's consciousness. His heart plummeted, crashing through the floorboards beneath his feet. Suicide? The word reverberated through his mind, an echo that refused to fade away.

"Are you sure?" Desperation laced his voice, a futile hope that there had been some mistake. With her quiet strength and wry smile, his sister couldn't be the subject of such a tragic event.

"Oliver, I wish I was wrong. There's... there was a note found by her side." Sheriff Coleman's voice trembled, the lines of duty and friendship blurring painfully. "She shot herself."

A cold numbness spread through Oliver, his body disconnecting from the present as shock took hold. Why would she do it? Hadn't they shared enough childhood hardships to forge an unbreakable bond? What pain had driven her to such despair?

"Oliver, are you there?" Jim's voice broke through the haze of disbelief.

"Y-yeah, I'm here," he stammered, struggling to anchor himself to the conversation. "It doesn't make sense. She would never do that. She...." His words trailed off, lost in the labyrinth of unanswered questions.

"I can come over, talk this through—" the sheriff

offered, the lines of his face etched with sorrow even through the phone.

"No, I... I need a minute, Jim." Oliver's voice was a hollow echo of his usual warmth. "Thanks for letting me know."

"Anything you need, Oliver. I'm here for you and your family."

With the call ended, Oliver stood motionless, the hum of the workshop now a distant murmur against the tide of his thoughts. The tools that once felt like extensions of his hands lay forgotten, their purpose momentarily insignificant compared to the turmoil raging within him.

He could feel the fibers of his being unraveling, each thread a question, a memory, a regret. His sister's laughter, her resilience, the way she could find light in the darkest of times—all these pieces of her clashed violently with the finality of her choice.

"Suicide," he whispered to the empty room, the word a stranger among his thoughts. Oliver's eyes closed, a silent prayer for understanding, strength, and the ability to navigate the storm of grief that threatened to engulf him. He clutched the phone as if it were a lifeline, the only connection to the sister he thought he knew, the sister he now realized he'd have to rediscover in her absence.

Oliver's hands were still trembling as he turned the ignition off, the truck's engine falling silent along with his racing thoughts. He needed guidance, something, or someone to anchor him in the tempest that had upended his world. Travis emerged in his mind—a beacon of wisdom and experience in the small town where everyone knew each other's joys and sorrows.

The walk to Travis's front door felt longer than it was, each step a leaden march through his uncertainty. The crunch of gravel underfoot seemed unnaturally loud in the quiet afternoon, a stark contrast to the turmoil within him.

Travis's house was a reflection of the man himself— unassuming yet resilient. The porch bore the burden of years, its wooden planks groaning softly as Oliver approached. The welcome mat, faded from countless seasons of sun and rain, lay before the door like a tired sentinel. It matched Oliver's mood—worn out by the harsh elements of life. Above him, the branches of an old oak tree swayed, their leaves whispering secrets to the wind that Oliver wished he could grasp.

His hand paused above the doorbell, a brief hesitation born from the dread of verbalizing the pain. It was one thing to know tragedy and another to speak it into existence. But this was Travis, a man who had weathered storms of all kinds, who—as a now retired cop— had stared into the abyss of human despair more times than most could bear.

Summoning the last vestige of his resolve, Oliver pressed the bell, its chime cutting through the silence surrounding the house. As he waited for the door to open, for the face of understanding to greet him, Oliver's heart thumped in his chest—not just with grief, but with the faintest flicker of hope that, in Travis, he might find a path forward through the darkness.

The door swung open, and there stood Travis, the evening light casting a golden hue on his tall, sinewy frame. His grizzled beard was like a bramble of wisdom, each strand seemingly earned through years of service and sorrow. His eyes, sharp and piercing as ever, held the calm of an ancient sea in a storm. With a nod, he stepped aside, the motion an unspoken invitation into his sanctuary.

"Come in, Oliver," Travis said, his voice deep and steady, a testament to countless conversations cushioned by gravitas and grace.

Oliver entered, his body moving mechanically while his mind spun with turmoil. The warmth of the house enveloped him like a gentle embrace, the interior walls adorned with photographs of Travis's past—a silent gallery of proud and painful memories.

"Sit down," Travis gestured toward an old, sturdy sofa that seemed to have provided comfort to many before him. "Tell me what's on your mind."

As Oliver sank into the cushions, the dam within him broke. Words tumbled out, raw and unchecked, painting the bleak picture of his sister's untimely departure from this world. His voice cracked as he recounted the sheriff's call, his hands animated with confusion and grief. The room felt heavy with the weight of his words, yet not suffocating—Travis's presence was like the steady hand of a lighthouse keeper on a tempestuous night.

"Trav, I just don't understand it," Oliver managed between breaths, his eyes wet with unshed tears. "We were close... even though we hadn't seen each other in ten years, we knew one another. She would have told me if something was wrong. She could have come to me. She knew this. Why would she... how could she...?"

Travis listened, his face a bastion of empathy carved from the bedrock of experience. He leaned forward slightly, giving Oliver the unspoken assurance that his pain was heard, his loss acknowledged. There were no interruptions, no platitudes, only the shared silence between two men—one seeking answers, the other offering a shoulder upon which those questions could rest, if only for a moment.

A tapestry of shadows danced across the walls in the dimming light, mirroring the tumult in Oliver's heart. Yet, amidst the chaos of emotions, the certainty in Travis's eyes offered a beacon of hope that perhaps, together, they could unravel the tangled threads of this tragedy. Feeling the first stirrings of catharsis, Oliver took a shuddering breath, clinging to the lifeline Travis extended simply by being present and understanding.

Oliver's chest heaved as he fought to steady his breath, the rawness of his emotions leaving him exposed in the quietude of Travis's living room. The older man had become a pillar in the storm, and now, as the silence stretched between them, Travis leaned back into his chair, the leather creaking under his weight. His voice was gentle and firm when it broke the hush, a testament to years of guiding others through their darkest hours.

"Oliver," he began, his gaze never wavering from the younger man's face, "you're standing at the edge of an abyss right now. I know the inclination is to shut out the world, but you need to do the opposite. You need to dive into her life and understand her days leading up to this."

Travis paused, ensuring his words took root. "Talk to her friends, find out where she has been. She must have had friends there, colleagues—anyone she's been around recently. They might hold pieces to this puzzle, insights into her state of mind that weren't apparent on the surface. You need to find out where she was and who she was with."

Oliver listened, each word from Travis acting as a suture to his frayed spirit. It was a direction, a course of action amidst the maelstrom of grief that threatened to consume him. Slowly, his hands unclenched, releasing his death grip on the armrests, as something akin to resolve began to take shape within him.

"But how do I do that?" he asked. "She just vanished. I've spoken to everyone she knew in town, and no one knows where she's been."

"Where was her body found? Maybe start there?" Travis said.

"Thank you, Travis," Oliver said, his voice steadier than before. His eyes, still brimming with sorrow, now reflected a flicker of determination. "I'll do that. I'll start first thing tomorrow." He paused, looking down at his calloused hands—hands that were used to shaping and fixing, yet felt so powerless now. "It just doesn't add up. She would've come to me and opened up about whatever was haunting her. We weren't close these past years, no, but I just know her."

Oliver's gaze returned to Travis, seeking guidance and validation for the turmoil raging inside him. "We used to be tight, you know? I thought we had each other's backs, no matter what. How desperate must she have been to see no other way out?" His voice cracked, the last words barely a whisper.

"I think your answer lies in why she left."

Travis reached across the space that separated them, laying a weathered hand atop Oliver's. The touch was grounding, a silent pledge of solidarity. "You may find answers you don't expect or even want, Oliver. But searching for the truth—that's how you honor her memory and get the answers you need to close this chapter."

As Oliver rose from his seat, his gratitude was a tangible force, a warmth spreading through his chest despite the chill of impending nightfall. He knew the path ahead would be fraught with heartache, but Travis's advice had ignited a spark within him, a drive to seek out the reality of his sister's final days. With a nod, a silent promise to himself and the man who had given him a lifeline, Oliver stepped toward the door, ready to embark on a journey where every answer would bring him closer to either solace or torment.

Oliver stepped out of Travis's house, the evening chill nipping at his skin as he pulled his coat tighter around him. The sun dipped low on the horizon, its last rays clinging to the day, casting elongated shadows that stretched across the path like dark fingers reaching out from the encroaching night. He paused for a moment, letting the scene etch itself into his memory—the way the fading light seemed to mirror the murky waters of uncertainty he was wading into. His sister's death was a puzzle, a shadowy labyrinth, and the truth lay hidden deep within its twists and turns.

The possibilities and questions swirled in his mind, forming and reforming into countless scenarios. What secrets had lain buried in his sister's heart? Who among her friends and acquaintances held the missing pieces that could explain the unexplainable?

As Oliver approached the familiar outline of his home, the warm glow from the windows stood in stark contrast to the creeping darkness that enveloped him. He pushed open the door and found Lisa in the kitchen, her silhouette haloed by the soft light above the stove. Her hazel eyes, always so full of warmth, now searched his face with concern.

"Travis thinks we should look into her last days," Oliver said, his voice a mix of resolve and sorrow. "There might be clues about... why she did it. He also thinks there might be a clue in finding out why she left."

He spoke of his sister, but it was Lisa's face he watched, seeking in her the strength he needed to anchor himself against the tide of grief.

Lisa crossed the room, her movements filled with the quiet grace that had first drawn him to her. She wrapped her arms around him, her embrace a fortress in the storm of his emotions. "You'll find out what happened," she whispered, her voice as resolute as the set of her jaw. "I truly believe you will."

Oliver nestled his face into the crook of her neck, allowing himself a moment to simply breathe in the scent of her, to let her presence soothe the raw edges of his heart.

"I just wish..." he began, then trailed off, the words catching in his throat.

"Shh," Lisa soothed, her fingers tracing gentle patterns on his back. "You don't have to do this alone, Oliver. I will be with you all the way and help you in any way I can. We'll uncover the truth together."

They stood there, in the heart of their shared life, bound by love and a shared determination.

The warmth of the kitchen wrapped around Lisa and Oliver like a comforting shroud, sealing away the chill of the small town's evening air. A hum from the refrigerator provided a soft backdrop to their silence as they stood in the heart of their modest home, enfolded in each other's arms. The steady rhythm of Oliver's heartbeat thrummed against Lisa's ear, a soothing counterpoint to the rapid flutter of her own.

With each shared breath, the space between them grew smaller until there was no distinction between where one ended and the other began. Lisa felt the strength of Oliver's arms, a testament to years of battling the sea and carving beauty from raw wood, now serving as her bastion of safety. She nestled closer, inhaling the familiar scent of sawdust and salt that clung to his flannel shirt—a smell that had long ago ceased to be just his but was now irreversibly interwoven with the fabric of their family.

"Oliver," Lisa whispered, her voice barely above the crackle of the stove where dinner simmered unattended. "The kids are at Maggie's tonight." Her words were delicate yet laden with an unspoken message that sent a thrill of anticipation down her spine.

She felt Oliver's body tense slightly, the shift almost imperceptible, reflecting the surprise and realization dawning within him. His hold on her tightened, a silent acknowledgment of the precious gift she'd presented— their brief escape from parenthood promised a fleeting return to the simplicity of being just Lisa and Oliver, man and wife, before life had layered them with titles and responsibilities.

"I thought we needed it," she continued, her eyes lifting to meet his gaze, revealing the depth of her vulnerability. It was a rare admission from a woman who had learned to wield strength as her armor, but here, in Oliver's embrace, she allowed herself the luxury of reliance, of sharing the weight that pressed upon her resilient shoulders.

Oliver's dark eyes sparkled with a mix of emotions, reflecting the heartwarming joy of unexpected freedom, tinged with the thrilling pulse of what that freedom could entail. A smile tugged at the corner of his lips, a silent vow that he, too, recognized the importance of this stolen moment.

In the quiet of the kitchen, where the aroma of their impending dinner mingled with the essence of their love, Lisa and Oliver stood on the threshold of rediscovery, holding each other tight, two souls intertwined.

Oliver's hands traced the contours of Lisa's back with a tenderness that belied his rough exterior. His touch, always so familiar yet endlessly thrilling, awakened a torrent of longing within her—a craving for closeness that transcended the physical. Her fingers, once adept at navigating through life's tumult alone, now danced across the fabric of his shirt, pulling him nearer as if their bodies could merge into one.

With every breath, every heartbeat, their embrace deepened, and the air around them was charged with the electricity of unspoken promises and shared histories. Lisa felt the world shrink to the space between them, a cocoon woven from threads of passion and interweaved destinies. She marveled at how Oliver's presence was both a safe harbor and an exhilarating storm, how he could stir waves of desire that crashed over her defenses, leaving her yearning for more.

A soft gasp escaped her lips as Oliver lifted her effortlessly onto the kitchen table with a strength borne not just from his physique but from a well of emotion. The wooden surface, which had borne witness to family meals and laughter, now supported a different kind of communion. Their lips met in a kiss that was a confluence of everything unsaid, a passionate declaration that spoke volumes in the room's silence.

The kiss was a dance, a duel, and a surrender all at once. Lisa's mind reeled with the intensity of it, the way Oliver's mouth moved against hers with a fervor that seemed to pull her deeper into his orbit. She wrapped her arms around his neck, drawing him closer still, their bodies engaging in a ballet of need and fulfillment. There was no beginning or end to their connection, only the continuous loop of their love, as seamless and eternal as the horizon line where sea meets sky.

Atop the sturdy table that bore the marks of their shared life, they rediscovered each other in that suspended moment. All the fears and uncertainties that haunted their small-town existence fell away, leaving a raw and beautiful urgency behind. It was heart-warming and thrilling, suspenseful and reassuring—their love story unfolding in the twilight of their kitchen, a testament to the enduring power of two hearts beating as one.

The aged pine table, an enduring fixture in the Thompson kitchen, groaned under the shifting weight of their fervent movements. The creaking wood, a rhythmic accompaniment to their racing hearts, seemed to echo the urgency that surged between Lisa and Oliver. It was as if the very fibers of the table understood the need to withstand this storm of passion—to hold together as sturdily as they did through all the chaos life had thrown at them.

Lisa could feel every solid inch of Oliver's woodworker's frame pressed against her, the strength in his arms offering a promise of safety as much as pleasure. Her fingers found sanctuary in the soft darkness of his hair, grasping lightly, then with growing desire as she pulled him closer. The texture was a familiar comfort that always anchored her in the tumultuous sea of their lives.

His lips journeyed from hers, charting a path of tender exploration down the column of her neck. Each kiss laid upon her skin was a spark that kindled deeper flames within—flames that only Oliver knew how to stoke. It wasn't just the heat of his mouth on her flesh; it was the knowledge that he understood her scars, both visible and hidden, and cherished her all the more for them.

As Oliver's kisses descended, each brush of his lips was a word in the silent language they shared, telling her of longing, love, and adoration. Lisa's breath hitched in the quiet of the kitchen, with the dusky light casting long shadows through the windows. She felt the fire inside her flare, consuming her doubts and fears, leaving in their wake a blazing trail of desire that only Oliver could navigate and quench with his touch, his presence, and his soul.

The thrill of their secret rendezvous, with the children safely away, heightened the intensity of the moment. Every sound—the sizzle of dinner forgotten on the stove, the whisper of their clothing, the deepening timbre of Oliver's breath against her throat—was magnified, adding layers of suspense to the unfolding drama of their romance. In this dance of love and longing, the stakes were high, the rewards immeasurable. They were both survivors, shaped by their pasts, yet here, in this moment, they found an exhilarating escape, a sanctuary of their own making.

Oliver's touch was a question and an answer, his body speaking to hers in a conversation too profound for words. And with each creak of the table, each gasp, and each entwined heartbeat, Lisa surrendered to the thrilling, heartwarming symphony of their love.

Oliver's palms traced the contours of Lisa's body with a craftsman's reverence. Each touch was a testament to his love, a balm soothing the memories of hardship etched in her skin. Once a bastion for family meals and laughter, the kitchen table bore witness to their unfolding ardor, its sturdy oak frame groaning softly beneath them.

Lisa arched into his touch, her hazel eyes darkening with desire. Moans spilled from her like secrets she'd kept locked away, each one a symphony to Oliver's ears, urging him on. His fingers danced across her ribs, slipping down to the small of her back where he knew she felt most vulnerable. With every caress, he seemed to be smoothing away the scars of her past, reaffirming their present entanglement of souls.

The world beyond the kitchen faded, its edges blurring into insignificance. There was only the rhythm of their breaths and the heat of their bodies moving in tandem. The space seemed to contract around them, the air charged with the electricity of their connection. Within these four walls, they crafted a refuge from the echoing silence of an empty house, from the ghosts that sometimes crept into their hearts.

With each movement, each shared heartbeat, they wove a tapestry of passion that defied the confines of their small-town existence. The kitchen—with its humming refrigerator, the ticking clock, and the soft glow of the overhead light—transformed into a temple where only they existed, where time held no dominion over the urgency of their love.

In this sanctuary, Lisa found strength in her surrender, an exhilarating freedom in the arms of the man who had anchored her once-drifting heart. The suspense of what each second might bring was over-shadowed by the thrill of knowing it was Oliver who stood with her at the precipice of ecstasy. Together, they reveled in the dance of their union, two survivors melding into one force against the world outside, their bodies and spirits moving in perfect, harmonious accord.

Oliver's breath warmed Lisa's neck, a stark contrast against the coolness of the kitchen table that pressed into her back. The windows were fogged, their view obscured by the intensity that radiated from within. Fingers entwined, they became the architects of an intimate world where every exhale was a whisper of yearning, and each touch weaved another thread into the fabric of their fervor.

The heady scent of their arousal rose, a tangible presence that wrapped around them like a veil. It danced with the aroma of herbs and spices sizzling on the stove, a symphony of smells that told the story of life lived deeply and passionately. The simmering pot was forgotten, its contents crackling in the heat as the dinner waited patiently and unobtrusively for the world to right itself again.

Lisa's heart pounded, a drumbeat syncing with Oliver's own as they moved together in a rhythm that became their unique language. Her hands clutched at him, nails grazing the woodworker's calluses that spoke of his labor and love. Their connection was a bridge across chasms of past pain, a testament to the resilience found in each other's arms.

Time, so often a thief, now granted them a rare gift. It stretched, allowing the lovers to chase the threads of their pleasure through the labyrinth of senses. The room shrunk until there was nothing left but the urgency of their bodies, the desperate pull toward completion that made muscles quiver and skin tingle with anticipation.

And then it happened—the crescendo of their desire crashed over them like a wave, relentless and all-consuming. Oliver's strong frame trembled, and Lisa's breath caught, her body arching as she met the surge of ecstasy that flooded through them both. They clung to each other, a pair of souls anchored amidst the tempest of release, riding the storm as it swept them up before gently depositing them back into the quiet afterglow of their passion.

In the stillness that followed, the only sound was the gentle ticking of the kitchen clock, counting seconds that had once been lost to the chaos of their love, now recovered and treasured within the walls of their sanctuary.

Lisa's chest rose and fell in a quiet rhythm, her breaths gradually finding their calm cadence after the tempest of passion that had swept through them. Oliver's arm cradled her back, his touch gentle yet still charged with the electric memory of their fervent union. The sturdy kitchen table beneath them felt like an island in a sea of tranquility, the wood warm from their heat.

A faint smile played on Lisa's lips as she listened to the soft hum of the refrigerator mingling with their synchronized breathing. The world outside the cozy warmth of their kitchen was laden with mysteries and silent threats, but within these walls, safety and love were the guardians of their shared moments.

Oliver brushed a stray lock of Lisa's shoulder-length brown hair behind her ear, his rough fingers a tender contrast to her soft skin. In the dimming light, her eyes held a galaxy of emotions, each one reflecting a chapter of their lives—the struggles they had faced and the strength they had drawn from one another.

Their gaze locked, and for a heartbeat, it was as though time paused, acknowledging the depth of their bond—a bond forged not just in the heat of desire but in everyday acts of resilience and devotion.

Leaning closer, their lips met in a tender and healing kiss, a balm for old wounds and a seal over new vows. It was a kiss that spoke of gratitude for the present and hope for the future, a kiss that was both an ending and a beginning.

In this intimate space, where the scent of their love was still potent, and the echoes of earlier laughter from Ethan, Abigail, Daniel, and even little Julia lingered, Lisa and Oliver found their sanctuary. They found a place where the heartbeats of romance and the pulse of a thriller converged—where every moment held the potential for a heartwarming connection or thrilling danger.

But for now, all was peaceful and still in the after-glow of their love. And that was enough.

Lisa's eyelids fluttered open, a languid smile curving her lips as she felt the synchronized rhythm of their heartbeats gradually ease into calmness. She shifted slightly under Oliver's embrace, her hands tracing the contours of his back, muscles still tensing and relaxing beneath her touch. The intensity of their connection resonated through her, a hum of energy that seemed to vibrate in the very air around them.

"Oliver," she whispered, her voice a soft murmur filled with lingering desire and contentment.

With care, he responded to her unspoken cue, his arms loosening around her as they began the tender process of disentangling their limbs. Their motions were slow, reluctant—as if parting from this union was an act against nature itself. Lisa's fingers grazed Oliver's cheek, and her touch was a silent testament to the raw passion they had shared.

As their bodies parted, the space between them was charged with the echoes of their intimacy. Still entwined at the soul, their physical separation was a gentle return to the reality of the life they had built together.

With a strength born from years of weathering tempests, both personal and literal, Oliver lifted Lisa from the table where they had been one entity moments before. Her legs dangled for a second, feet searching for the solid ground that seemed so far away after soaring to such heights together. His hands were there, steady and sure, as he guided her descent.

Once on the firmness of the kitchen tiles, Lisa's body swayed ever so slightly, still adrift in the aftershocks of their love. Oliver's fingers remained interlaced with hers, a lifeline connecting them. Together, they turned toward the stove, where the aroma of a simmering dinner promised another kind of nourishment.

"Let's eat," Lisa suggested, her voice still husky. Her hazel eyes reflected the flickering flames beneath the pot, hinting at the fire that remained unquenched within her.

"Sounds perfect," Oliver agreed, his deep voice resonating with the silent vow to protect this moment, to guard the sanctuary they had created against any storm that might loom on the horizon.

Side by side, they approached the stove, the warmth from the bubbling dinner mingling with the warmth still radiating from their skin. In the quiet of the kitchen, with the dusk painting strokes of color outside their window, they found solace in the simple act of being together, ready to savor the quiet intimacy that was theirs alone.

Lisa reached for two plates, her movements languid and unhurried, still feeling the remnants of bliss tingling on her skin. She handed one to Oliver, their fingertips grazing, sending a shiver down her spine that had little to do with the coolness of the porcelain. A soft chuckle escaped her, the sound mingling with the hiss and pop of the cooking food.

"Be careful," Oliver said with a low chuckle, "or we might never get to dinner."

She gave him a playful glance, but her eyes danced with the same warmth that had ignited between them moments before. As they filled their plates, the clinking of cutlery against ceramic served as a gentle reminder of the world beyond their cocoon of intimacy—a world that waited patiently for their return.

They moved to the small kitchen table, a trusted witness to their family's laughter and tears. Pulling out chairs, they sat close enough for their knees to touch beneath the table, an innocent contact that resonated with the promise of more. The simple wooden surface, scarred from years of use, held their meal—a hearty stew that carried the scent of thyme and rosemary, of home and heart.

Oliver took Lisa's hand in his, his rough carpenter's fingers speaking volumes against her softer skin. They shared a look that conveyed a thousand unspoken words, a lexicon of love that needed no translation. He squeezed her hand gently, a silent thank you for the sanctuary they'd built within these walls, far from the shadows of their pasts.

"Every time with you feels like the first," Lisa whispered, the emotion evident in her voice. Her gaze held a mixture of gratitude and wonder, the kind that comes from finding a love both unexpected and fiercely protective.

The room was filled with a tranquility that belied the undercurrent of excitement and anticipation for what lay ahead. In the corners of the room, shadows gathered, hinting at the thrill of secrets yet to be unraveled, of dangers lurking just outside the safety of their haven. But within the glow of the overhead light, those threats seemed distant, unable to reach the fortress of their bond.

As they ate, each bite tasted of something more than the spices and ingredients; it was seasoned with the essence of their connection, a flavor that no chef could replicate. They savored each mouthful, the silence comfortable, filled only by the occasional scrape of a spoon or a contented sigh.

"Tomorrow's another day," Oliver said, the phrase a subtle reminder of the challenges they faced, the responsibilities that awaited them beyond the kitchen door. His blue eyes held a determined spark that spoke of his readiness to face whatever the world threw their way, so long as he faced it with Lisa by his side.

"Tonight," Lisa replied, leaning her head against his shoulder, "let's just be us."

"Us" was a word that encompassed everything they were together—lovers, partners, and guardians of a precious family. It was a declaration, a battle cry, and a prayer all at once. And in that quiet kitchen, as night pressed its nose against the windowpanes, "us" was all they needed.

Oliver pulled away from Lisa's embrace with gentle firmness and walked over to the aged oak desk that had once belonged to his grandfather while she cleaned up from dinner. The surface was cluttered with wood shavings and sketches of his latest designs, remnants of his life before tragedy sliced through it. His hands, rough from years of coaxing beauty out of raw timber, swept aside the debris, clearing a space for a different kind of work now.

He took out a fresh notebook, the spine cracking as he opened it to the first page—a blank canvas awaiting the map of his sister's hidden world. Oliver jotted down names, each an anchor point in the sea of her life: childhood friends, even those fleeting acquaintances who might hold a stray piece of the puzzle. Each name was a step on the path Travis had illuminated, a potential key to understanding the why that haunted him. Someone had to have spoken to her. Someone had to know where she was and where she went after leaving town. She had to have contacted someone at some point. Right?

With every name recorded, his plan solidified, transforming from nebulous grief into a tangible course of action. He would start tomorrow, visiting each person, listening to their stories, searching for the unspoken truths lurking between their words. It was detective work, plain and simple, though he was no detective—just a brother driven by love and loss, seeking answers in the wake of an incomprehensible act.

"Oliver?" Lisa's voice pulled him back from his thoughts, her tone threaded with concern.

He looked up at her, his eyes reflecting the flicker of resolve that Travis's counsel had sparked within him. "I've got a list," he said, tapping the notebook. "People who knew her and places she frequented when she still lived here. It's time I learned what was happening in her life that led to... this. If I can only find out where she has been, maybe there is an answer for me there."

Lisa nodded, her eyes mirroring his determination. "We'll start first thing in the morning."

The room seemed to contract around them, the walls pressing in with silent questions and secrets yet to be uncovered. But within Oliver, something else was expanding—a sense of mission, a drive that went beyond merely coping with his sister's death. He felt it as a thrumming energy in his veins, a readiness to confront whatever lay ahead.

Standing, he moved toward the window, the street lamp outside casting long shadows across the floor like dark fingers reaching out toward him. He watched the horizon and took a deep breath.

"Whatever it takes, I'll find out why." The words left him with a quiet intensity, a vow spoken not just to Lisa or himself but to the very essence of the universe that had dared to take his sister without reason.

"Whatever it takes," Lisa echoed, joining him by the window, her hand finding his and squeezing tightly. "Let's go to bed now."

"I'll be up in a few minutes," he said.

Lisa left, and Oliver turned from the window, his gaze steadfast and his posture that of a man who knows the road will be treacherous yet walks it anyway. He was ready to delve into the labyrinth of his sister's life, chasing down every lead and memory until the truth could no longer be hidden.

With a final look around the room that held so much of his former life, Oliver Thompson braced himself for the journey ahead. The determination in his eyes was clear, the line of his jaw set. There were answers out there, scattered like breadcrumbs through the forest of the past, and he would follow them until they led him to the clarity he sought—the clarity his sister deserved. Satisfied with his decision yet troubled by the grief, he poured himself a glass of whiskey to calm his nerves. When that glass was gone, he poured himself another one.

Chapter Five

The rustic scent of aged paper and wood shavings mingled in the air of the dimly lit workshop. Oliver, his rugged hands now still, sat amidst a chaos of memories splayed across his heavy oak desk. The glow of a solitary desk lamp cast elongated shadows as he leaned closer to scrutinize an old photograph—a Polaroid image of his sister laughing, her eyes bright with life. He traced the edges of the picture with a calloused fingertip as if trying to reach through time itself. In the box next to him were hundreds of other photos from their childhood, along with all of Michelle's old things, which his parents allowed him to go through in his search for answers.

"Oliver?" Lisa's voice, warm and laced with worry, cut through the silence. She stood at the threshold, leaning slightly against the door frame, her figure soft yet resilient, like the light from the hallway that battled the room's gloom. Her eyes, usually so full of warmth, now held a storm of concern as she watched her husband lose himself in his search for answers.

"Hey," Oliver replied, not looking up, his voice barely more than a whisper lost among the whispers of the past.

"'The kids are in bed," she said, tentatively stepping into the workshop. It wasn't just a place of crafting and creation; it had become a sanctuary for Oliver's grief, a refuge where he could chase the ghosts that haunted him. You've been here since dinner... Maybe it's time to rest?" Her suggestion hung between them, delicate and fragile.

Oliver's gaze remained fixed on the pictures, his jaw set, the muscles twitching as he wrestled with unseen adversaries. He had talked to more than a dozen of her old childhood friends and acquaintances these past few weeks, and no one could tell him anything about where she went or even why she left. It was a mystery to all and a surprise when it happened. She was simply just gone, they said.

"I can't, Lisa. There's something here, something we all missed. I need to find it."

Lisa moved closer, her presence a gentle force in the room, strong enough to stand against the tides of despair that threatened to consume him.

"I know you want to understand what happened to her, but this—" She gestured to the disarray of his makeshift investigation, "—this isn't healthy. It's been weeks now. You're not sleeping, you're hardly eating, and when you look at me, I feel like you're a thousand miles away." Her voice trembled with emotion, each word saturated with care.

"It's like she's still calling out for help, Lisa," Oliver murmured, his voice thick with sorrow. "And I wasn't there for her."

"Oliver, love, we're here now, your family—me, Ethan, Abigail, Julia, and Daniel. We need you here with us."

Lisa reached out, laying a hand on his shoulder, feeling the tension coiled within his muscles. "Your sister would have wanted that too, wouldn't she?"

His body seemed to sag under the weight of her touch, a silent admission of his inner turmoil. The mask of determination slipped for a moment, revealing the raw anguish beneath. Oliver tilted his head back, finally meeting Lisa's gaze, the torment in his own eyes mirrored by the pain in hers.

"Promise me you'll come to bed soon?" she asked softly, her plea a lighthouse beckoning him back from the stormy sea of his obsession.

Oliver nodded, a mute vow to try, even as the relentless tide of unanswered questions pulled at him. They both knew the gravity of the situation—that their small town idyll was fraying at the edges, a thriller playing out in real life, with the stakes being their family's very heart.

With a final squeeze of his shoulder, Lisa retreated, her silhouette fading into the hallway, leaving Oliver to his vigil. The photographs and memorabilia whispered secrets just beyond his grasp.

A week later, the clock ticked past midnight in the dimly lit study. Shadows danced across the walls as the flickering flame of a lone lamp illuminated Oliver's furrowed brow. He shuffled through the scattered memorabilia with fervent intensity, each photograph a puzzle piece that refused to fit. The air was thick with the musty scent of old paper and the sharp tang of whiskey that clung to his breath.

"Oliver," Lisa's voice sliced through the silence like the peal of church bells on a quiet Sunday morning, startling him. She stood at the doorway, her silhouette framed by the soft yellow light from the hall, watching him with an ache in her hazel eyes.

"Lisa, I can't stop now. There's something here—I can feel it." Oliver's words were steel wrapped in velvet, his resolve unyielding despite the late hour.

"Darling, you've been at this for weeks. It's consuming you." Her approach was cautious, the floor-boards creaking underfoot as she entered the room. "And the drinking—it's not helping. It's just—" Lisa stopped short, catching herself before saying too much.

"Not helping? You think I don't know that?" His voice cracked, a hairline fracture in his otherwise sturdy demeanor. "But this pain inside me, it drowns me without the booze. I need to numb it to keep going, to find closure."

"Oliver, please." The plea was raw, her own pain surfacing. "Think about Ethan, Abigail, Julia... Daniel.

They're seeing you like this, broken, always with a bottle in your hand. We can't let that be their memory of their father."

He slammed his palm against the desk, the sound echoing, a punctuation mark to his frustration. "They need to remember me as someone who didn't give up on family! Someone who sought the truth, no matter the cost."

"Is the truth worth more than your health? Our children's happiness? Your life with me?" Lisa's voice trembled, but her conviction was steadfast.

"Without the truth, none of it means anything!" Oliver roared, his face a mask of anguish. "Can't you see that?"

"Oliver, look at me." Her command was gentle but firm. She took his hands in hers, the calluses of his woodworker's touch familiar and comforting. "You're not alone in this. But we need you whole, not shattered and lost to these shadows. Let's find help together."

He looked down at their entwined fingers, a lifeline amidst the storm of his grief. In that instant, the scales tipped—the weight of his sorrow pitted against the unwavering strength of her love. Oliver was a man adrift, but even now, he could sense the pull of the safe harbor she offered.

Her heart pounded with fear and hope as she held his gaze, searching for a sign of the man she loved within the tempest. Would he choose the warmth of her embrace or the cold comfort of his solitary quest?

"Okay, Lisa. Okay." His voice was barely above a

whisper, a surrender to the concern glinting in her eyes. It was a start, a tiny crack in the armor he had built around himself these past weeks. But it didn't last long.

The warmth of his affirmation had been short-lived, fading as quickly as the amber liquid in his glass. It was a week later, and Oliver still seemed lost. He spent every evening in the office, looking at old photographs and not getting anywhere. Lisa watched as Oliver lifted the bottle again, his hands steady despite the tremors that rattled her own nerves. The twilight cast long shadows across their kitchen, a once cozy space now tainted by the specter of loss and addiction.

"Oliver," she tried, her voice a blend of tenderness and exasperation, "you said you'd consider getting help."

He scoffed, pouring another drink with a precision that betrayed his frequent practice.

"I can manage, Lisa. It's not like I'm falling apart at the seams."

His chuckle was hollow, echoing against the walls adorned with family photos—their smiles a stark contrast to the tension that hung between them.

"Please," she implored, her gaze begging him to see reason. But he only turned away, his silhouette rigid against the windowpane.

"Look around, love. This," he gestured vaguely, encompassing the room, the house, their life, "is how I cope. My sister is gone, and this"—he raised the glass to his lips—"numbs the pain. It's my burden to bear." The words fell heavily into the silence, each one a nail in the coffin of his denial.

Lisa's heart ached, recognizing in his stance the same stubborn resolve that had drawn her to him. But where there was once passion and conviction, now there was only a desperate clinging to the ghosts of the past.

Retreating to the bedroom, she pulled out her phone and dialed Maggie, the ringtone cutting through the quiet with an urgency that mirrored Lisa's pulse. When her friend's voice answered, warm and familiar, it was all Lisa could do to keep her own from breaking.

"Maggie, it's me," she whispered, her words quick and hushed. "I don't know what to do anymore. Oliver's drinking... it's getting worse. He won't listen to me. He says it's his way of dealing with things, but I'm scared. For him, for the kids...."

There was a pause, and then Maggie's calm assurance filled her ear. "Sweetheart, you're doing everything you can. But you have to think about your children too. They need a stable environment, especially now."

Tears blurred the edges of Lisa's vision, and she wiped them away with a shaky hand. "I know, I just... I thought if we loved him enough and surrounded him with care, he'd come back to us."

"Love is powerful, Lisa, but it's not always enough to fight someone else's demons," Maggie replied softly. "Sometimes they have to face those on their own.

You've got to protect yourself and those kids first and foremost."

"Thank you, Maggie. I'll... I'll figure something out."

Lisa hung up the phone, her decision heavy in her chest. There was no thrill in the prospect of confronting the man she loved, no excitement in the suspense of the unknown road ahead. Only the heartwarming certainty that she would do whatever it took to keep her family safe.

The afternoon sun spilled across the kitchen table, igniting the amber hues in Lisa's hair as she sat, a steaming mug of coffee between her palms. The usual comforting aroma couldn't ease the knot in her stomach, nor could the warmth seep into her trembling fingers. She gazed out the window, where golden leaves danced in the breeze, whispering of change.

"Lisa?" Maggie's voice was gentle but firm, pulling her back from the whirlwind of thoughts. They had been talking for hours now, with Lisa revealing the depth of the hardship she was going through, which had been going on for two months. Oliver's drinking was getting worse, and he was absent as a husband and father. His need for answers had become an obsession, and it was tearing them apart.

"You know I wouldn't say this if I didn't believe it was necessary. I love you guys. I love your family. But right now, you are struggling. He's dragging you all down. For you and for the kids... it might be time to put some distance between you and Oliver, at least for a little while. Show him you mean business if he doesn't change."

The suggestion hung in the air, heavy and daunting. Lisa's heart lurched at the thought, her love for Oliver battling against the cold grip of fear that had taken residence in her chest.

"Separate?" The word felt foreign on her tongue, tasting of betrayal and abandonment. "But he's my husband, Maggie. In sickness and in health, right?"

"Of course," Maggie reached out, her hand warm over Lisa's. "But this sickness is hurting all of you. Setting boundaries doesn't mean giving up on him. Think of it as... stepping back to see the whole picture."

Lisa's mind raced, images of their life together flickering like an old film reel—the laughter-filled days at the café, Oliver helping little Julia learn to walk, or having her in his lap while doing woodwork, his arms wrapped around her in the quiet of the night. How could she untangle those memories from the recent nights filled with shouting and fear?

"Oliver loves us," Lisa whispered, more to herself than to Maggie. Her hazel eyes were stormy with doubt. "He's just lost right now."

"Lost or not, you can't let him pull you all down with him." Maggie's voice was steady, a lighthouse amidst the tempest raging inside Lisa. "Think about Ethan, Abigail, Daniel, and Julia. They're looking to you to keep them safe. You can all stay with me. I have this whole house to myself, and I'm not even here half the time. I'm always at the tavern."

A vision of Ethan, wide-eyed and confused after one of Oliver's recent outbursts, flashed before Lisa. The mother lioness within her roared to life, protective instincts overpowering the doubts that chained her to inaction.

"Okay," Lisa breathed, a tremulous sigh that held the weight of her world. "We'll stay with you for a while. Just... until things get better."

"Good." Maggie squeezed her hand, a silent symbol of solidarity. "I'm here for you, always. You're not alone in this."

As Lisa stood, resolve settling over her like armor, the last rays of sunlight kissed the edge of the horizon, setting the sky aflame. The beauty of the moment wasn't lost on her; even as her heart ached, it was buoyed by the thrilling spark of hope that came with taking control.

She'd fight with everything she had, a fierce love guiding her through the suspenseful unknown. Oliver's demons would not claim her family, not if she had anything to say about it.

The evening air was heavy with the scent of pine and an impending storm when the sharp crack of Oliver's voice sliced through the tranquility of their home. "You just don't understand, Lisa! I have to do this—for her, for me!"

Lisa's heart pounded in sync with the thunder that grumbled in the distance, a tempest brewing within her as she faced her husband. His eyes were wild, a turbulent sea reflecting his inner turmoil, and she knew at that moment that her decision could no longer be postponed.

"Oliver, please," she implored, her voice steady despite the chaos swirling around them. "Think of Ethan, Abigail, Daniel, and Julia... think of us."

But his gaze was fixed on the faded images of his lost sister, a silent testament to his obsession.

"I am thinking of them!" he shot back, his fists clenched at his sides. "I'm trying to protect them from making the same mistakes!"

"By destroying yourself? By drowning in a bottle?" Her words were pointed, laced with fear and frustration. This wasn't the man she married—the tender-hearted woodworker who had once carved their initials into the old oak by the creek. This was someone else, someone consumed by grief and guilt.

"Mommy?" The small, quivering voice cut through their heated exchange like a knife. Abigail stood at the foot of the stairs, clutching her stuffed rabbit, her large eyes filled with uncertainty.

"Sweetie, go back to bed. Everything's okay," Lisa said, though her voice betrayed her assurance.

"Go!" Oliver's command was ragged, his hands

running through his hair in despair. "Just go if you're gonna leave! Don't wait until tomorrow. Leave."

The words hung in the air, suspended like the final note of a sad song. Lisa's resolve solidified as she gathered her courage like a cloak around her. With a glance that conveyed the depth of her love and the agony of her choice, she whispered, "I'm so sorry, Oliver."

In a flurry of motion, Lisa ushered the children, half-asleep and confused, into their jackets. She collected the essentials—diapers for Julia, a few clothes, the dog-eared copy of her favorite Harry Potter book that Abigail couldn't sleep without—and herded them toward the door.

"Lisa, you can't do this!" Oliver's plea was a mix of anger and desperation, his frame silhouetted against the flickering light of the living room lamp.

"Please, get help, Oliver. For your family," she urged, her voice breaking as she opened the door and stepped into the uncertain embrace of the night.

Oliver, muscles tense and jaw set, watched helplessly as the love of his life disappeared into the shroud of darkness with their children. He wanted to chase after them and beg for forgiveness, but his feet remained rooted, and his heart shattered piece by piece.

"You're not thinking straight!" he called out, voice hoarse, even as the car's taillights vanished down the winding road. "Lisa!"

But there was only silence and the distant rumble

of thunder in response. Alone, he turned to face the empty home, each room echoing with memories and ghostly laughter. The haunting realization that his actions had driven them away settled heavily upon him, and the first drops of rain began to fall as if the heavens themselves wept for what had been lost.

The key turned with a soft click in the lock, and Lisa gently pushed open the door to Maggie's home. She stepped inside, ushering her children into the warmth that seemed to be infused with an immediate sense of security. Maggie was at the tavern but had left the lights on, the glow from the living room casting a welcoming beacon in the otherwise shadowy night.

"Mommy, are we going to stay here?" Ethan's voice was small, tinged with confusion and sleepiness.

"Just for tonight, honey," Lisa assured him, brushing a kiss on his forehead as she set Julia down in the portable crib Maggie had prepared. Abigail clutched her book close to her chest, eyes wide and searching. Lisa reached out, smoothing her daughter's hair and trying to muster a smile that felt genuine.

"Everything will be okay," she whispered, more for herself than for the children. The weight of her decision pressed on her shoulders, but here, at this moment, there was a semblance of peace.

Meanwhile, Oliver sat at the kitchen table,

surrounded by an eerie stillness that seemed to mock him. The half-empty bottle of whiskey stood before him like an old friend who whispered false promises of forgetfulness. He poured another glass, his hands shaking slightly as he did so. Each gulp burned its way down, but it couldn't sear away the guilt that gnawed at his insides.

He looked around the once vibrant space, now devoid of laughter and light. The empty chairs were tombstones marking the absence of his family, and the ache in his chest grew with each labored breath. Oliver slammed the glass down, splintering the quiet with the sharp sound. It was all his fault. The realization was a bitter pill, one that no amount of alcohol could sweeten.

"Lisa...."

Her name escaped his lips, a whisper lost in the expanse of their deserted home. He rose unsteadily, wandering through the rooms where his children's imaginations once ran wild. Their drawings still adorned the refrigerator door, and the colorful scribbles and stick figures were in stark contrast to the monochrome grief that filled the house.

"Come back," he pleaded to the shadows, to the memories that lingered just out of reach. But there was no answer, only the oppressive cloak of loneliness that threatened to suffocate him. He stumbled back to the bottle, the only companion left to him in this self-made purgatory.

Outside, the rain intensified, pounding against the windows with a ferocity that matched his inner turmoil. Lightning flashed briefly, illuminating the despair etched deep into Oliver's face. He didn't notice the storm; he was already drowning in a tempest of his own making.

Lisa sat at the kitchen table in Maggie's house, her laptop open before her. The soft glow of the screen was a beacon in the pre-dawn quiet, the only light in a room shrouded in the stillness of early morning. Her fingers danced across the keys with purpose, each click a step toward a solution. She scoured the internet for local support groups and counseling services, her hazel eyes scanning through pages of resources with a resolve that belied the turmoil inside her.

"Mommy?" A small, sleepy voice broke the silence. Lisa turned to see Abigail rubbing her eyes as she padded into the kitchen.

"Hey, sweetie," Lisa said, her voice a soothing whisper. She scooped Abigail into her arms and kissed her forehead, feeling the heavy weight of responsibility on her shoulders. "Couldn't sleep?"

"I miss Ollie," Abigail mumbled, snuggling into her mother's embrace.

"Me too, baby. Me too."

"Will he be okay without us?"

Lisa's heart clenched, but she held herself steady

for her daughter. She knew what she had to do, not just for the children but also for Oliver.

"Let's get you back to bed," Lisa whispered, rising from the chair with Abigail clutched close. She walked down the hallway, the patter of the rain outside a rhythmic accompaniment to her thoughts. Once Abigail was tucked in and drifting back to sleep, Lisa returned to her research with renewed urgency.

The sun began to peek over the horizon as she finally closed her laptop, a list of potential lifelines for Oliver compiled. Support groups for addiction, grief counseling sessions, even a nearby rehab facility—each one a beacon of hope in the engulfing darkness of Oliver's depression.

Her heart raced at the thought of confronting him, of pushing past the barricades he'd erected around himself. But this wasn't just about them; it was also about Ethan, Abigail, Daniel, and Julia. She had to be strong for all of them.

She decided then to go back the next day. She needed to face Oliver and show him there was a path forward if only he would take the first step with her.

"Oliver needs to understand that I'm doing this because I love him," she murmured, a mix of determination and dread churning within her. The possibility of change, of redemption for their fractured family, was thrilling in its own right. Yet it was heart-stopping, too, knowing everything hinged on the conversation that awaited her.

She would bring Oliver back from the brink, not

just for their sake but also for his own. She made this promise to herself, her children, and the man she loved, no matter how lost he seemed.

"Tomorrow," she whispered, the word a vow filled with suspenseful hope, "everything starts tomorrow."

Chapter Six

The creak of the door was softer than a whisper as Lisa stepped into the dimly lit living room. Her gaze immediately found Oliver, her husband, stretched out on the couch. His chest rose and fell with the deep rhythm of slumber, oblivious to the world around him. Sunlight fought its way through the half-closed blinds, casting long shadows over the scattered remnants of last night's solitude—a sea of empty beer bottles that stood testament to Oliver's inner turmoil.

Lisa's heart clenched at the sight, a familiar cocktail of worry and love stirring within her. She glanced at his face, peaceful in sleep, his dark hair tousled against the armrest. It was a stark contrast to the rugged hands that once skillfully navigated both fishing nets and wood grains, now lying limp by his side. In these quiet moments, she could almost forget the painful family history that haunted him, the invisible burden he bore that seemed to grow heavier with each passing day.

With practiced care, Lisa set down her purse and began the silent ritual of cleaning up. She maneuvered between the coffee table and the couch, retrieving bottles with grace borne from years of navigating the unpredictable waters of her first marriage. The clink of glass echoed softly as she placed them into the recycling bin one by one. Each movement was a silent offering of support, a hope whispered through action that this time might be different—that the tides would turn and carry Oliver back to safer shores.

As she gathered the last of the bottles, her mind replayed the countless times they had danced this dance. The thrill of their love and the suspense of not knowing what each new day would bring was part of the fabric of their shared existence. And yet, amidst the heartbreak, there was an unyielding determination in her eyes—an unwavering resolve that she would not let the storm claim the man she loved without a fight.

Lisa paused, looking down at Oliver again. His face, usually animated with laughter or furrowed in concentration while working on his latest woodworking project, now betrayed the signs of his battle with the demons of his past. She wanted to reach out, to smooth the worry lines from his forehead, but she refrained. Instead, she focused on the task at hand, allowing the familiar rhythm of tidying up to steady her own racing heart.

With the last bottle tucked away, she stood still for a moment, taking in the quiet aftermath. Lisa knew that when Oliver awoke, the real work would begin—the gentle nudging, the difficult conversations, the delicate balance between confrontation and compassion. The café, their shared dream, would open soon, and with it, another day filled with the possibility of change.

For now, though, she let the silence wrap around them like a comforting blanket, holding onto the hope that love, above all, would guide them through the storm.

Lisa moved to the kitchen, her movements a silent dance as she reached for the coffee pot. The rich aroma of ground beans filled the air, a scent that always seemed to bridge the gap between despair and a fresh start. She watched the dark liquid trickle into the carafe, each drop a promise of clarity and a nudge toward sobriety. Her hands were steady as she poured the steaming coffee into his favorite mug—the one with the faded anchor on the side, a nod to Oliver's days at sea.

She took a deep breath and carried the cup back to the living room. The morning sun peeked through the curtains, casting a warm glow over Oliver's slumbering form. Lisa's presence was a quiet beacon as she knelt beside the couch, her closeness a whisper of hope in the stillness.

"Oliver," she said softly, her voice laced with warmth yet carrying an undercurrent of urgency that the morning could no longer wait. His name was a prayer on her lips, a call to rise above the tempest that brewed within him.

With the patience of the tide returning to shore, she touched his shoulder, her fingertips conveying her resolve along with the tenderness that only love could foster. There was a moment of suspense, where time seemed to hang suspended, waiting for him to respond, to acknowledge the world beyond his troubled dreams.

"Hey," she continued, the single word tender but laden with expectations. "I made you some coffee. It's time to wake up."

The mug, placed within his reach, became a silent testament to her faith in him, a symbol of the normalcy they both desperately craved. The steam rose, carrying with it the unspoken messages of her heart—messages of concern and hurt but also of unwavering companionship.

Oliver's eyelids fluttered, a grimace contorting his features as the vestiges of sleep were chased away by reality's harsh light. He shifted on the couch, his body protesting with a symphony of aches that resonated in his bloodshot eyes—a crimson map of the night's excesses. The stark paleness of his skin stood out against the shadows that clung to him like specters of regret.

Lisa bit down on her lip, a fortress against the sorrow welling up inside her. She watched Oliver's struggle, every line of fatigue etched into his face serving as a reminder of the battles he fought within. His disheveled hair and the stubble lining his jaw spoke of a neglect that extended far beyond the physical, reaching into the depths where once the steady flame of resilience burned bright.

The room was silent, save for the soft tick of the clock on the mantle—a metronome to their life's unsettling rhythm. The tension hung heavy, an unspoken question lingering in the air between them. Would today be different? Could the warmth from her steadfast heart thaw the cold grip of his affliction?

Lisa's heart ached, the weight of shared dreams and whispered promises bearing down on her chest. She fought back tears, refusing to let them fall, her strength a bulwark against the tides of despair threatening to breach her resolve. Her love for Oliver, a beacon in their tempest-tossed world, refused to be extinguished by the storms he summoned around himself.

In the quietude of that moment, Lisa's presence— full of hope yet tinged with fear—blended with the morning light that now pooled around them, casting a hopeful yet uncertain glow upon the day's canvas. Oliver's slow and pained awakening might just be the first step toward redemption or the prelude to another day lost to shadows. Their future, balanced precariously on the fulcrum of this fragile dawn, awaited his choice.

The scent of freshly brewed coffee sliced through the stale air, a silent herald of the morning's cold truth. Lisa set the steaming mug on the worn wooden table, its soft clink a punctuation in the stillness of their home. She perched on the edge of the couch, her gaze tracing the lines of exhaustion that etched themselves into Oliver's face.

"Oliver," she began, her voice steady despite the turmoil that raged within her. "Why are you doing this to yourself?" The words hung between them, charged with a desperate hope for clarity.

He blinked, the bloodshot orbs seeking focus. For a moment, there was silence as if the question stirred something deep and long-buried within him. But then, the walls came up, his expression hardening like the crust of ice on a winter lake.

"Maybe I just enjoy my own company more than others," Oliver retorted, a bitter edge to his words. His eyes moved away from her, focusing instead on a crack in the plaster on the opposite wall as though it held answers she could not provide. "Or maybe you don't have to stick around if it bothers you so much."

It was a shield thrown up in haste, a deflection from the pain that gnawed at his insides—a pain he knew all too well but refused to acknowledge.

Lisa's breath hitched, her heart warring with the urge to reach out and the knowledge that he might push her away. Her spirit cried out to heal the rift between them. Oliver's words stung, but they also unveiled the depth of his struggle, the fight that lay ahead, and the love she knew was worth every scar it may leave upon her heart.

Lisa's resolve solidified as she looked down at the man whose heart she knew was a labyrinth of love and pain. She knelt beside him, her hand trembling as it found his, the roughness of his woodworker's calluses brushing against her skin. Tears welled in her warm hazel eyes, not out of pity but born from a wellspring of love that refused to run dry despite the drought of their recent days.

"Oliver," she whispered, her voice laced with a strength that belied the moisture glistening on her cheeks. "I can't pretend to understand the ghosts you're fighting or the demons that drive you to seek solace in these bottles. But I do know this—our love is not a casualty of these battles. Not if we don't let it be."

Her words were a lifeline cast into turbulent waters, hoping he'd grasp it and pull himself ashore.

She brushed a stray lock of hair from his forehead, the intimacy of the gesture a stark contrast to the distance that had crept between them. The room was still, filled only with the sound of her soft breathing and the occasional shifting of Oliver on the couch.

"Tonight, the kids and I will come back home. They miss their father; they need you, Oliver.... We all do," she continued, her voice gaining momentum, cutting through the silence like the first rays of dawn piercing a night sky. "And I want to believe—no, I need to believe —that you'll be here waiting for us, not just in body but in spirit too."

Lisa's tears fell freely now, tracing paths along her cheeks as her heart held onto a fragile hope.

"This might be your last chance to change, to fight back for the life we've built together. We still have hope. Don't let it slip away, Oliver. Don't let us slip away."

The air hung heavy with her declaration, an unspoken ultimatum wrapped in the tenderness of a woman who had weathered storms yet still navigated by the stars of her love. Her gaze never wavered from his face, searching for a sign, any indication that her words had reached him, that they had ignited a spark in the darkened room where he lay.

"I have found... places that might help. We can look at them together and see what might work for you. I will help you, my love. Through every step of your recovery."

For a brief, heart-stopping moment, Lisa saw the flicker of something vulnerable and raw in Oliver's eyes before he closed them again, retreating to whatever refuge he sought in sleep. But she had said her piece and laid her heart bare before him, offering both a lifeline and a challenge. Now, it was up to him.

Lisa stood motionless, the weight of her words still reverberating in the air. Oliver's silence was a vast chasm between them, filled with the echoes of their past and the quiet ticking of the clock on the mantel—a reminder that time was slipping by. She studied his face, searching for a hint of the man who once chased sunsets with her, whose laughter was the melody to which her heart beat. But the lines of his features gave nothing away, his eyes closed to her plea.

The quiet was oppressive, yet within its depths, Lisa clung to an unwavering belief—an ember of hope that stubbornly refused to be extinguished. She saw the strength that had carried Oliver through storms at sea, the tenderness he reserved for their children, the love that had once been unshakable. It was there, she assured herself, somewhere beneath the haze of alcohol and regret. He would find his way back; he had to.

Shaking off the uncertainty that threatened to unravel her, Lisa straightened her shoulders, a silent promise etching itself into her resolve. The tears that had cascaded down her cheeks now felt cold against her skin as she wiped them away, each one a testament to the battles they had faced together. This was not the time for surrender—it was the hour for courage and faith in the vows they had made in the presence of family and friends.

With resolute steps, she moved through the home that bore the marks of their life together—framed photographs that whispered of happier times, hand-prints on the walls from little fingers that had explored every nook and cranny. The familiar creak of the floorboards under her feet was a comforting cadence as she pulled on her apron, the armor of normalcy she donned each day.

Today, like every day, she would open the café, grind the beans, steam the milk, and greet the regulars with a smile that reached her eyes. And perhaps, just maybe, today would be the day that Oliver would push through the swinging doors, sober and clear-eyed, ready to mend the fractures in their shared existence.

As she walked down the stairs to their café, the town slowly waking around her, Lisa held onto the thrill of possibility, the suspense of the unknown. Her heart warmed at the thought of Oliver sitting beside her once more, crafting wood into art as he used to, the scent of sawdust mingling with the aroma of coffee. A future where fear and doubt were replaced with trust and healing stretched out before her, tantalizing in its potential.

She unlocked the door to the café, flipping the sign to "Open" with a flick of her wrist. The bell above the door would jingle with the entry of each patron, and Lisa hoped, with every fiber of her being, that Oliver would join her—he was her partner in life, her co-conspirator in love. For now, she would wait, serve, and smile, the heartbeat of the small town steady and reassuring even as her own raced with anticipation for what the day might bring.

Chapter Seven

Lisa perched on the edge of a creaky chair behind the counter, the scent of freshly ground coffee beans mingling with the undercurrent of unease that never quite left her. The café hummed with its usual afternoon lull, patrons engrossed in their world of whispers and the soft clink of porcelain. Her fingers, marked by tiny scars of resilience, drummed against the wood, betraying her inner turmoil. Oliver hadn't come down to join her as she had hoped. Instead, she heard him leave a few hours earlier and had no idea where he was going. It filled her with worry. But she hadn't given up hope. She cast a furtive glance over her shoulder, ensuring prying eyes were occupied before hurrying into the back office.

The box of memories Oliver had been so obsessed with going through was inconspicuous and frayed at the edges, as though it had journeyed through time itself. Lisa's heart, usually so steady and warm like the hearth of their family home, now galloped with a blend of trepidation and resolve. She opened the lid with a steadiness she didn't feel, revealing its secrets. On top was a photograph stained by age but safeguarded by memory.

Oliver's youthful grin was unmistakable, his protective arm slung around a younger girl. Lisa's hazel eyes softened for a moment, touched by the innocence of the young siblings. Oliver was in his early twenties; Michelle was in her late teenage years. This had to have been taken shortly before she disappeared. But as she peered closer, the quaint image turned sinister. Behind them stood a figure, barely discernible among the shadows of an old oak tree. It was not just a trick of the light or the whisper of an old tale; it was the outline of someone watching, lurking.

Her pulse quickened, and she leaned in, scrutinizing every inch of the grainy background. The figure seemed deliberately concealed by the dappling sunlight, its presence an enigma that clawed at the corners of her mind.

With each ragged breath, courage swelled within her chest, warming her veins with fear and adrenaline. The photo trembled in her grasp, yet Lisa's determination was unyielding, and the peculiarity of it all ignited a fire in her belly.

Fingers flying over the keyboard, Lisa's relentless pursuit of truth echoed in the rhythmic tapping. The café, usually a sanctuary of warmth and chatter, now felt like a silent accomplice to her secret investigation.

She toggled between tabs, scanning line after line of digitalized newspaper archives. The glow of her laptop screen cast an eerie luminescence on her face, accentuating the resolve etched into her features.

"Come on; come on," she muttered under her breath, as if coaxing the secrets to rise from the depths of the internet. Hours trickled by unnoticed, the steady hum of the coffee machine in the background a distant reminder of the world outside her growing obsession.

Then, amidst the blur of headlines and dates, something caught her eye—a ten-year-old article that seemed to pulse with significance. Her heart hitched as she clicked on it, bringing the faded print to life against the backlight of her screen. "Local Woman Vanishes Without a Trace." The headline was stark, the story beneath it chilling in its brevity.

Lisa read it once, twice, and thrice, the words blurring together as the implications became clear. It described a young woman, Michelle Thompson, beloved by the community, who had disappeared on a warm summer night, leaving behind only questions and a haunting absence.

Her mind raced, piecing together memories Oliver had shared, the cause of death—suicide—he'd recounted with a pained voice. None of it aligned with the narrative laid out before her. The photo—Oliver's sister, carefree and smiling, with that shadowy figure in the background—was a stark contrast to the hollow emptiness suggested.

"What happened to you, Michelle?" she whispered

into the quiet room, feeling the weight of betrayal beginning to tinge her confusion. The air around her grew heavy and thick with the scent of roasted coffee beans and the burden of secrets untold.

She took a deep, steadying breath, her mind alight with the kind of heart-pounding excitement that precedes a great unraveling. With each new detail unearthed, the path ahead loomed, fraught with danger and the promise of a love tested by fire. Resolute, Lisa braced herself against the swell of emotion, ready to confront whatever truths lay hidden in the shadows of the old oak tree and beyond.

The timbers of the cozy kitchen seemed to shrink back, absorbing the shockwaves of raised voices that ricocheted off well-worn countertops and family photographs lining the walls. Lisa's eyes, usually alight with warmth, were now aflame with a different fire as she faced off against Oliver, his dark hair tousled from running his hands through it in frustration. It was evening now; all the kids had returned from school, and Julia was back from daycare. She had told them all to come back to their home, that they would stay there tonight, hoping things would be better. But they weren't. She was now holding a bottle of whiskey, which Oliver had just poured a drink from after returning home, sneaking in through the back door while she was cooking dinner. She had walked into the living room to show him the picture and ask him about the guy when she found him drinking again.

"Oliver, this is not what we agreed on!" Lisa's voice cracked, but her stance remained firm even as her heart raced—a familiar echo of past fears threading through the present confrontation. "I told you to stay sober. For us."

"Dammit, Lisa! You just don't understand," Oliver shot back, his broad shoulders heaving, an outward manifestation of his inner turmoil. The muscles, honed from years of wrestling with the sea and smoothing wood into art, now tensed in readiness for a battle of a different kind.

His hand, which had so often tenderly caressed the curve of her cheek or guided their children's small fingers around the grip of a hammer or chisel, now balled into a fist. And in a moment that stretched too long, like a deep breath before a plunge into icy waters, Oliver slammed that fist onto the table with a force that made the room shudder.

Lisa's heart skipped a beat, and instinctively, she flinched. A single step back was all her body allowed, compelled by the muscle memory of a time when such gestures foretold real danger. Yet even as she moved away, her resolve rooted her to the spot, a lighthouse steadfast in stormy seas.

The argument hung suspended for a heartbeat, a tableau of tension and unspoken fears. In that flicker of silence, the scent of sawdust and the comforting aroma of coffee that always lingered in their home became a stark contrast to the electric charge of the moment, reminding them both of what was at stake.

"Oliver, please," Lisa implored, her voice a raw edge of desperation that cut through the thick atmosphere. Her eyes were pools of worry as she reached across the divide that had formed between them, her hand trembling slightly in mid-air. "This isn't just about us. It's hurting the kids; can't you see that?"

The words seemed to hang for a moment, suspended in the tension that filled the room. Lisa watched Oliver's shoulders heave with each breath, his jaw set hard like the wood he so lovingly crafted. She knew this man, knew the kindness and love that lay beneath the stormy surface, and it broke her heart to see him like this, to see their family threatened by the rising tide of his anger.

From the corner of her eye, Lisa caught a movement—a slight shift of shadow that drew her gaze toward the doorway. Ethan stood there, wide-eyed and protective as he wrapped an arm around Abigail's shoulders. Their faces were mirrors of confusion and fear, painted with the innocence of youth suddenly thrust into the adult world of conflict. Behind them peeked Julia, clutching her teddy bear. Her one-year-old mind was unable to comprehend what was happening but was sensing the distress all the same. And at the back, Daniel's sensitive blue eyes reflected a depth of emotion that belied his six years, a silent witness to the fracturing of his once-secure world.

"Look at them, Ollie," Lisa's voice cracked,

gesturing toward their children. The plea was not just for understanding but for the reclamation of the warmth they all desperately needed.

"They're scared. We promised to make a safe place for them, away from... from all the things we've seen. We can't let that slip away from us."

Ethan's jaw tightened, mimicking his stepfather's as he edged forward, his green eyes flickering between the two adults. Abigail's small hand found its way into his, seeking solace in the familiar comfort of her brother's presence. Even as the scene unfolded before them, the bond between the siblings was a tangible force, a tiny ember of hope amidst the chill of uncertainty.

The room held its breath, every heart beating to the rhythm of suspense and the unspoken question that lingered in the air: What would happen next? Would Oliver heed the call of his family's love, or would the shadows of his past prove too powerful to overcome? In the balance hung the fragile threads that bound them together, each one quivering with the weight of a future yet undecided.

The tremor in Lisa's heart echoed the quiver of the handmade wind chime that hung forgotten on the porch outside, its melody lost to the storm brewing within the walls of their once tranquil home. Oliver's shadow loomed large over the kitchen table, his voice a thunderclap that made the room shrink.

"You think I don't know what this is doing to us?" Oliver's words were a snarl, his frustration boiling over as he turned the blame upon her like a knife twisting. "You're always trying to fix things, Lisa. But not everything is under our control!"

Lisa watched, her hazel eyes reflecting the pain of his accusations. The love that had always been their compass now seemed adrift in dark waters. His refusal to see his part in the tempest left her isolated on an emotional island, his words sending ripples through the fragile atmosphere.

"Ollie," she whispered, the name a plea, but his gaze was impenetrable, a fortress built from years of guilt and introspection.

From the corner of her eye, Lisa saw Ethan's form stiffen, the boy bracing against the tension like a young tree facing a gale. Abigail's grip on his hand tightened, her small frame trembling with each raised word. Julia and Daniel stood like statues, their innocence a stark contrast to the charged air between their parents.

No, she couldn't let it come to this. Not again.

With every fiber of resolve woven into her being, Lisa stood taller, her posture firming against the onslaught of Oliver's misplaced anger. Her voice carried a new weight when she spoke again—a mother's determination to shield her cubs at all costs.

"Oliver, this isn't just about us anymore." The steel in her tone surprised even herself. "I won't let them grow up walking on eggshells, wondering if today is the day when their father's temper will—"

"Enough!" The word cut through the air, a line drawn that could not be uncrossed.

But it was enough. It was enough for her to realize that the safety and happiness of Ethan, Abigail, Julia, and Daniel were her paramount concern. They deserved more than whispered apologies and the echoes of slammed doors.

Her love had always been a beacon, strong and powerful, lighting the way. Now, it was time to harness that love, to turn it into action—for her children and herself. Oliver's face, etched with conflict, was both a map of the man she loved and the terrain of trials she must now navigate away from.

As the argument dwindled to a simmering quiet, Lisa's resolve did not waver. She would find them a haven where laughter was the soundtrack, not raised voices—where the only shadows cast were those of play beneath the sun's gentle rays, not the darkness of anger in their own home.

She would do it for Ethan's furrowed brow, Abigail's seeking hand, Julia's bewildered eyes, and Daniel's silent plea. Deep down, she knew she would also do it for Oliver—for the man he once was and the man he might still become if left to face his own storm head-on.

The decision settled in her chest, a stone of certainty amidst the shifting sands of doubt. It was a course charted by necessity, love, and survival. Oliver might not join her on this voyage, but she would set sail nonetheless, her precious cargo too valuable to leave behind in troubled waters.

Lisa blinked through a film of tears, her vision sharpening as she scanned the room that had once been a sanctuary of love and laughter. Each piece of furniture, each worn path in the carpet, bore silent witness to the life they'd built. But now, it all spelled out the need for escape.

She drew a steadying breath, her fingertips tracing the cool metal of the pendant at her neck—a talisman of strength she hadn't removed since the day Oliver gave it to her. That Lisa—the one who believed challenges were just tests of love—was fading into the shadows of this decision. The new Lisa, the one standing in the eye of the storm with unwavering determination, focused on the safe harbor ahead.

"Mom?" Abigail's voice was a thread of uncertainty that tugged at her resolve.

"Sweetheart," Lisa murmured, kneeling to meet her daughter's gaze. We're going back to Aunt Maggie's to stay for a while—not just for one night this time. It'll be like an adventure, okay?"

Abigail nodded, her small hand trusting in her mother's. Lisa straightened her back, a commander of her own destiny, her heart galvanized by the trust in her child's eyes.

She moved from room to room, gathering clothes,

toys, and the essentials of their lives with swift efficiency. Each article placed into the suitcase was a step toward their newfound future: a soft teddy bear that Daniel couldn't sleep without, Abigail's beloved sketchpad filled with dreams too vibrant for their current reality, Ethan's schoolbooks—all found their place among the fabric of their transient home.

The packing was systematic and purposeful; there was no time for sentimentality. The sun dipped lower, casting long shadows across the walls, reminding her that twilight would soon fall. Their window to leave, under the veil of dusk, was narrowing.

In the quiet of the bedroom, Lisa paused, her hands hovering over the drawer that held Oliver's sweaters. She could almost feel his arms around her, sweeping away the chill of fear that had crept into her bones. With a shuddering breath, she closed the drawer. Not everything could be salvaged.

"Ready, Mom?" Ethan's voice, edged with the weight of understanding beyond his years, pulled her back to the present.

"Almost," she whispered, offering him a smile that promised brighter days.

Lisa zipped the last bag closed and lined them by the door, a testament to their readiness to embark on this unforeseen journey. Her heart throbbed with a mingling of sorrow and adrenaline, but she refused to let the former overpower the latter.

"Let's go, my little warriors," she said, her voice

steady despite the tremors that threatened to shake her foundation.

They filed out, a parade of quiet resilience, leaving behind the echoes of a life that could no longer contain them.

❦

Oliver stood in the doorway, his silhouette framed by the flickering porch light, his face a canvas of raw emotion. Lisa faced him, the children huddled behind her like small, guarded sentinels. The air between them was charged with the electricity of unspoken words and stifled feelings, the years of love and turmoil mingling in their shared breaths.

"Lisa, please...." Oliver's voice cracked, reaching for something beyond the chasm that had opened between them.

"Oliver, please move out of our way," Lisa replied, her voice a whisper-thin thread of strength. Her eyes held a glint of resolve that bordered on defiance. "The kids need peace. I need... we need a fresh start."

Her words hung between them, each syllable heavy with the weight of finality. Oliver's hands clenched and unclenched at his sides as if grappling with an invisible adversary. He took a halting step forward, then stopped, the battle within him etched in the tense lines of his body.

"I know I've messed up," he admitted, his words

laced with the sting of self-reproach. "But I can change, Lisa. For you. For them."

His gaze swept over the faces of Ethan, Abigail, Julia, and Daniel, each one a reflection of the life they'd built together.

Lisa felt the pull of their history, the countless moments of tenderness and laughter that had been their foundation. But underneath lay the fault lines of Oliver's unchecked temper, the dark undercurrent that had slowly eroded their trust.

"Change has to come from you, Oliver, for you," she said, her heart constricting with a pain that was both sharp and freeing. "Maybe then... maybe then we can find our way back to each other."

She saw the hope flicker in his eyes, a vulnerable spark amidst the shadows. With a soft sigh, she stepped forward and wrapped her arms around him in a bittersweet embrace, feeling his warmth for what might be the last time.

"Goodbye, Oliver."

"Please... Lisa... no...."

With those final words, Lisa turned away, a silent tear trailing down her cheek. She guided her children to the car, buckling them into their seats with hands that trembled not from fear but from the magnitude of the step she was taking. As the engine came to life, she cast one last look at the home that had once been their safe harbor, now just a repository of memories too painful to hold onto.

The car rolled down the street, its headlights

cutting through the darkness of the night, illuminating the path ahead. Lisa gripped the steering wheel tightly, and the road unfolded before her like a story yet to be told. The weight of her decision pressed down on her, yet a buoyant sense of relief bloomed within her chest.

The headlights of Lisa's car pierced the veil of night as she navigated through the winding streets, her destination a beacon in the darkness. Pulling into the driveway, she killed the engine and sat for a moment, gathering herself. The silhouette of Maggie's house loomed before her, its windows glowing with the promise of sanctuary.

With a deep breath, Lisa unsnapped her seatbelt and glanced back at her children, their faces serene in slumber. She stepped out into the cool air, each step toward the front door quickening her pulse with anticipation and an undercurrent of suspense. What would this new chapter hold?

Before her hand could even graze the handle, the door swung open. Maggie stood there, her curly hair framing her face like a lion's mane, eyes shining with unspoken understanding. Without a word, she enveloped Lisa in a hug that seemed to absorb all the tremors of uncertainty that had rattled Lisa's bones for so long. It was more than an embrace; it was an affirmation that the road ahead, while unknown, was not one she would have to navigate alone.

"Come in; come in," Maggie whispered, her voice a soft lullaby against the turmoil of Lisa's thoughts. "You're safe here."

Inside, the warmth of the house wrapped around them like a blanket. As Lisa gently woke the children and led them through the threshold, they blinked sleepily, taking in the cozy living room adorned with knick-knacks and framed photographs that spoke of happier times. There was a hum of life within these walls, a stark contrast to the sterile tension that pervaded their own home.

"I kept your rooms ready for you," Maggie said, guiding them down the hallway. Her touch was light on the children's shoulders, but it carried the weight of steadfast support. The beds were neatly made in each room, plush toys lay atop pillows, and night-lights cast a soothing glow. For the first time in months, Lisa felt her shoulders relax—here was stability and peace.

As the children settled into their temporary haven, Lisa moved through the motions of unpacking, her hands steady now. Ethan, Abigail, Julia, and Daniel watched her with quiet curiosity, their young minds trying to piece together the puzzle of this abrupt shift. Lisa met each of their gazes with a smile that didn't quite reach her eyes but promised that everything would be okay.

Maggie busied herself in the kitchen, the clinking of pots and pans a comforting soundtrack to their new beginning. The aroma of something sweet and savory wafted through the air, a tangible thread of normalcy that tethered them to the notion of home.

"Let's eat," Maggie called out, her voice infused with cheer. At the table, they gathered, a makeshift family forged by necessity and bound by love. Laughter soon bubbled up, tentative at first, then growing bolder as the meal progressed. In this space, Lisa allowed herself to exhale fully, her watchful eyes softening as she took in the scene—their resilience amidst upheaval.

Later, when the children nestled into their beds, whispers of dreams lacing their breaths, Lisa lingered at the doorway. Maggie joined her, a silent sentinel.

"Thank you," Lisa murmured.

"Anytime," Maggie replied, squeezing Lisa's hand. "We'll figure this out. I don't want you to feel like a burden. I mean what I have said. You can all stay as long as you need and want to. I'll always be here for you."

The moon hung high as Lisa retired to her room, its silver light spilling across the quilt that hugged her frame. With every beat of her heart, a quiet thrill pulsed through her veins—a thrilling blend of fear and hope for what tomorrow might bring.

In the silence of Maggie's house, Lisa closed her eyes, and for the first time in a very long time, she dreamed not of escape but of beginnings.

Oliver stood at the threshold of the darkened kitchen, his gaze tracing the contours of the empty chairs and barren table. A single plate, his own, lay untouched, dinner congealed and forgotten. He flicked the light switch; nothing happened. The bulbs had burned out days ago, another detail he'd neglected. Shadows loomed large in the corners of the room, mirroring the growing void within him.

The deafening silence pressed against his ears, starkly contrasting the cacophony of laughter and arguments that once filled the space. Each echo of the clock's tick was a sharp reminder of the family that was no longer there to ignore its persistent rhythm. Their absence was tangible, heavy in the air like a thick fog, suffocating him with the weight of realization.

He descended into the living room, where toys were scattered—a battleground of memories. Julia's doll lay face down as if mirroring his defeat, while Daniel's wooden blocks, those he had crafted himself during countless evenings of shared creativity, spelled out disjointed words. They seemed to accuse him now, each letter a testament to opportunities squandered.

Sinking onto the couch, Oliver buried his face in his hands, the roughness of his calloused palms a testament to a life spent shaping wood but failing to mold his own actions. An image of Lisa's tear-streaked face surfaced, her resolve as she shielded their children, and the sting of her departure sliced through him anew.

"Enough," he whispered into the void, his voice barely piercing the enveloping hush. It was a plea to the universe, a vow to himself. Oliver knew he'd hit rock bottom when the very foundation he prided himself on protecting—his family—had crumbled by his own doing.

His heart hammered with an unfamiliar fervor, an urgent call to action. He rose, pacing like a caged animal, finally recognizing the confines of its self-made prison. Oliver stopped by the fireplace, fingers tracing the mantel where photos of happier times stood. Dust had gathered, but beneath it, the smiles of his wife and children still shimmered with life.

"Time to face the demons," he muttered, determination hardening in his gut. His reflection in the cold, dark window pane revealed nothing of the man he used to be and everything of the man he needed to become.

With purposeful strides, Oliver climbed the stairs to the attic, where old boxes housed the ghosts of his past. Cobwebs clung to his sweater as he rummaged through the relics of a troubled childhood, confronting the echoes of anger and regret that had haunted him for years. He unearthed the leather-bound journal his therapist had given him, long abandoned but now held like a lifeline.

Returning downstairs, he sat at the desk that had once been the epicenter of his woodworking designs. He opened the journal to the first blank page, the pen poised above it trembling slightly. This was where he would carve out a new beginning and etch out a plan to rebuild the trust he had shattered.

Words started to flow, each sentence a pledge, a

blueprint for change. He wrote of accountability, therapy, and patience. He wrote of unyielding and unconditional love, the kind he owed to Lisa and the children.

As dawn painted the horizon with hues of forgiveness, Oliver sealed the envelope containing his written promises. He placed it on the mantle, a covenant on display, a testimony to his commitment. Outside, the world began to stir, and within the walls of the empty house, so did a glimmer of hope. Oliver Thompson, the man who had known the depths of despair, was ready to reclaim his life, to fight for the warmth of family once more.

Chapter Eight

Lisa's fingers danced with a rhythm born of urgency across the brittle pages of an old newspaper, each word and image scanned with meticulous care. The library's silence enveloped her as she delved deeper into the archives, a guardian of forgotten tales. In this hallowed quiet amidst the scent of ancient paper and ink, her heart leaped—a small column on the bottom corner of the page spoke of a sighting.

"Local Hiker Claims Encounter with Woman from Missing Person's Case," the headline read, and Lisa's pulse quickened as she absorbed the details. According to the article, the hiker had been traversing the rugged trails of the nearby mountain range when he stumbled upon a woman whose appearance bore a striking resemblance to the one in the faded photograph of Oliver's sister that Lisa kept folded in her wallet.

The woman's description—her hair the color of autumn leaves, eyes that captured the hues of the forest after rain—mirrored the memories Oliver had shared on long, sleepless nights. A surge of hope blossomed within Lisa, warm and invigorating like the first rays of dawn piercing through an endless night. This could be the lead they had been searching for, the breakthrough that would save her marriage, save Oliver from his demons.

With hands that trembled ever so slightly, Lisa scribbled down the hiker's name: Jameson Clark. She googled him and found his contact info. This Jameson Clark might hold the key to unlocking the mystery that loomed over their family, and Lisa felt the weight of possibility press against her chest.

She clutched the notebook to her heart for a moment, allowing herself to bask in the potential of this newfound clue. There was a fire within her, a flame kindled by love and fortified by resilience—the same flame that had seen her through her own dark days and now promised to illuminate the path ahead.

"Jameson Clark," she whispered, the name a vow upon her lips. She would reach out, unearth the story behind the encounter, and chase down every shred of evidence with the tenacity of a woman who had learned that the only way to keep her family safe was to confront the shadows head-on.

Closing the archive with gentle reverence, Lisa glanced at the clock. Hours had passed, but time was a mere construct when it came to matters of the heart. With the lead secured and her spirit alight with an intoxicating blend of anticipation and resolve, she prepared to step back into the world outside—one step closer to unraveling the enigma of a disappearance that had haunted them all. Hopefully, it would help get Oliver back to being himself again.

The bell above the café door jingled as Lisa strode in, her breath forming soft clouds that mingled with the rich scent of ground coffee. The familiar, comforting buzz of conversation and clinking dishes wrapped around her like a warm embrace, but her mind was elsewhere, churning with the potential breakthrough she had just uncovered. Marianne, their now full-time employee, greeted her with a big smile and a huge "Hi Lisa." It had been a week since Lisa had been there—since she left with the children, but she was happy to see that the café was still doing well.

The question was whether Oliver was.

Lisa maneuvered through tables of patrons, her eyes searching until they landed on the woodwork shop adjacent to the café. There, amidst the sawdust and the golden glow of afternoon light streaming through the windows, was Oliver. He stood at his workbench, sand-papering a piece of cedar with hands that told tales of years spent at sea, now tenderly shaping wood.

Lisa felt her heart race in her chest.

"Oliver," Lisa called softly, not wanting to startle him.

He looked up, his gaze locking with hers, and

everything else fell away for a moment. His presence was a steady anchor, and the fact that his eyes were clear and his stance sure—signs of his sobriety—fueled an indescribable warmth in her chest.

"Hey," he said, setting down his tools as a gentle smile graced his rough-hewn features. "Everything okay?"

"Better than okay," she replied, her voice a mixture of excitement and nervous energy. She approached him, the evidence of their past struggles and shared resilience reflected in the way they instinctively reached for each other's hands. "I found something—a lead."

Oliver's brow furrowed with intrigue as he wiped his hands on his apron and gave her his full attention. This was the man she loved and trusted, the one who had weathered storms both literal and metaphorical by her side.

"Tell me," he urged, his pulse quickening with the gravity of the moment.

Lisa unfolded the copy of the article she had brought, laying it gently on the workbench. As Oliver leaned over to examine it, she recounted the details: the hiker, the mountains, the woman who could be Michelle.

"Here," she pointed to the part where the hiker described the woman he'd seen.

Oliver's eyes scanned the lines, widening as the implications hit him. A myriad of emotions flickered across his face—hope and fear danced a delicate tango as he absorbed the words.

"Could it really be her?" he whispered, almost to himself.

"It's the best lead we've had so far, Oliver. I spoke to Detective Ramirez, who has looked through the case for me, and this is in the same area where her body was found in a cabin. He gave me the location of the cabin so we could go check it out, like Travis suggested. And I wrote down the hiker's contact information. We can reach out to him and ask him about what he saw that day, even though it was ten years ago," Lisa said, her fingers trembling slightly with the weight of the possibility before them.

Oliver straightened up, the craftsman's precision in his movements now replaced by an intensity that mirrored Lisa's determination. In his eyes, she saw the reflection of all their shared dreams and the silent fears that lurked in the quiet hours of the night.

"Are you sure you want to do it?" he asked. "After everything that has happened?"

She smiled, then nodded. "Yes. It might be good for us."

"Okay, then, let's go," he said, the resolve in his voice matching the unwavering strength she knew so well. "Let's find out the truth about what happened to Michelle."

Their shared resolve hung in the air, palpable and potent. The thrill of the chase, the drive to uncover hidden truths, and the hope of bringing closure to a long-standing wound in their family's heart converged in this single, heart-stopping moment. Lisa fully believed this could heal their marriage, and there was nothing she wanted more. Seeing Oliver sober had given her new hope.

Together, they stood in the woodwork shop, surrounded by the comforting scent of cedar and the tangible evidence of Oliver's craftsmanship. But their minds were already journeying beyond the safety of their small town into the rugged expanse of the mountains that held secrets waiting to be unearthed.

Lisa's fingers worked methodically, folding clothes into a duffel bag with an efficiency born from years of motherhood. Her mind raced as she mentally checked off the essentials they would need for the trip into the mountains. Already in the garage, Oliver was loading up his old truck with camping gear and provisions, the clatter of equipment punctuating the urgency of their mission.

"Lisa, do you think Maggie would mind watching the kids while we're gone?" Oliver called out, his voice tinged with concern.

"Already asked her," Lisa replied, her voice steady despite the fluttering in her stomach. "She insisted, said it'd be her pleasure to have them. I told her we didn't know how long we would be gone, but she didn't mind, she said."

Maggie, ever the guardian angel of their small community, had become family in all but blood, especially over the past week when Lisa had been living in her home. Lisa knew that, with Maggie, the children would be more than just looked after—they would be cherished. Hopefully, once they returned, they could be a family again and move back into their home.

With the car packed, they shared a brief, charged glance, each acknowledging the weight of what lay ahead. Both of them were happy to be together once again. Lisa was happier than ever to see Oliver's blue eyes clear and sober.

The engine roared to life, and they pulled away from the familiarity of home and headed toward the unknown.

As the town's quaint houses gave way to open road, Lisa felt the tension easing from Oliver's shoulders, his hands less white-knuckled on the steering wheel. Their conversation turned to Michelle, Oliver's lost sister. Each memory surfaced like precious gems—her laugh, so like Oliver's; the way she could spin a tale and have them all believing in magic; her adventurous spirit that seemed to beckon her toward the wilds of the mountains.

"When she was little, she used to hide in the woods, saying she'd found a fairy ring. It would scare the heck out of our mom," Oliver said, a faint smile curving his lips.

Lisa nodded, her hazel eyes reflecting the sunlight

that streamed through the canopy of trees lining the road, while Oliver continued:

"And we'd all go looking for her, only to find her sitting there, serene as anything, convinced she'd seen the fair folk."

They laughed as Oliver told the stories, each story a piece of the puzzle that had been jumbled and incomplete for far too long. It wasn't just about discovering what happened to Michelle or unraveling the mystery; it was about healing a wound that had marked Oliver and his family for years.

The drive stretched on, winding roads leading higher into the embrace of the mountains. The air grew cooler and the wilderness more pronounced, enveloping them in its untamed beauty. It was easy to imagine how someone could disappear here, swallowed by the vastness.

"Whatever happens," Lisa said, her hand finding Oliver's as he drove, "we're doing this together. We'll face whatever we find, just like we've faced everything else."

Oliver squeezed her hand in response, his blue eyes reflecting a storm of emotions. Hope, fear, determination—all etched into the lines of his rugged face.

"Together, forever and always," he echoed, the promise binding them as tightly as the rings on their fingers.

The mountain peaks loomed ahead, majestic and daunting, but Lisa felt only the thrumming excitement of a challenge to be met head-on. They were a team again, unbreakable in their unity, and as the miles disappeared behind them, the anticipation of discovery propelled them forward into the heart of the mystery.

The crunch of gravel gave way to the soft pad of earth as they stepped onto the trail, the boundary line between the known and the unknown. They had driven as far as they could until the road ended, and now they had to hike the rest of the way to the cabin. Lisa could feel the chill of the mountain air seeping through her jacket, invigorating and pure. Each breath was like a new beginning, each exhalation a release of city life's tight grip on her lungs.

With steady hands, she pulled out the worn leather-bound notebook that had become her constant companion in recent weeks. The pages were filled with hastily scribbled notes, maps sketched in moments of inspiration, and now they would hold the details of this journey. Her fingers traced the pen over paper, detailing the curl of ferns along the path, the mossy stones that served as silent trail markers, and the occasional deer track that crossed their own.

"Look at this," Oliver murmured, pointing toward a hawk circling above. "She's hunting—just like us."

Lisa glanced up, a small smile tugging at her lips. "Let's hope we're as successful as she is," she said, returning the focus to her notebook. They continued in silence, save for the symphony of nature around them—

the rustle of leaves, the distant call of birds, and the whisper of the wind through the pines.

It wasn't long before the forest seemed to close around them, the trees standing tall and dense, guardians of the secrets within their domain. Time lost meaning as they moved deeper into the wilderness; the world was reduced to the space of light and shadow that surrounded them.

Then, as the afternoon began its slow descent into evening, something caught Lisa's eye—a dark shape that seemed out of place amidst the sea of the forest. She tugged at Oliver's sleeve, her heart quickening.

"Over there," she whispered, her voice barely rising above the sound of a nearby stream. "Do you see it?"

Oliver followed her gaze, squinting against the dappling sunlight. "That must be the cabin?" he guessed. A sense of unease settled over them both. This was where Michelle had taken her own life, according to the police report. She shot herself in the head and left a note simply stating:

I can't do it anymore. Goodbye.

Together, they veered off the main trail, pushing through brambles and low-hanging branches until they stood before the structure. It was an old cabin, seemingly abandoned, its wooden planks weathered and gray. A shiver ran down Lisa's spine—not from the cold, but from the realization that this forgotten place might hold the key to the questions that had haunted them.

"This is the last place Michelle was," she breathed,

the possibility hanging between them like a tangible thing.

"Could be a hundred years old," Oliver countered, though his voice lacked conviction. He was trying to derail the conversation and not think of his sister in her last hours. The thought was simply too hard. His eyes scanned the clearing, searching for any sign of recent activity, but all he could see was the police tape fluttering in the wind.

"Let's check it out," Lisa said, determination edging her words. There was no room for hesitation; they had come too far to turn back now. She stepped forward, unconsciously reaching for the notebook in her pocket —her shield and record against the unknown.

Oliver nodded, and together, they approached the cabin, each step measured and cautious. The door hung slightly ajar, inviting or warning; they couldn't be sure. But as they crossed the threshold, the sinking sun cast long shadows across the forest floor, and the cabin awaited them, silent and still, a mystery within the mountain's embrace.

Dust motes danced in the slanted light as Lisa's fingers traced the edges of a Polaroid photograph. Lisa had found it inside a book left on the nightstand by the bed. It wasn't until she lifted it up that the photo fell out. The picture was a candid shot, a moment frozen in time of Michelle, Oliver's sister. And it was a recent one. She was visibly older than in the others Lisa had seen her in.

"Look at this, Ollie," Lisa whispered, passing him the photograph. Her heart constricted as she watched his hands, strong and capable from years spent carving wood, shake slightly as he took it.

"Michelle...." His voice trailed off, a mixture of wonder and sorrow. The image was undeniable—here was a piece of her, a clue that screamed relevance amidst the dust and shadows of the long-abandoned cabin.

Oliver drew closer, his presence a comforting warmth at her side as they pored over the photo together. This sharing of discovery felt intimate as their heads bent close, fingers brushing occasionally. Their connection deepened with every revelation, the search for his sister's last moments forging an unspoken bond that melded their determination and hope.

"She must have been here for a longer period," Lisa said. "The police took all her belongings as evidence, but the report said that her suitcase was here, and her clothes were on hangers. You only hang up clothes if you plan to stay for more than just a day or two, right?"

"You're making a good point," he said. "Do you think she was alone?"

Lisa held up the photo she had found inside the book. "Not at all. Someone took this photo. It was taken here inside the cabin; you can see the fireplace in the background."

"You're right. She couldn't have been here alone then," he said. "Maybe she was meeting someone here."

"A secret love, perhaps?" Lisa stared at the photo and then realized something. "Give me my phone, please."

He handed her purse to her, and she pulled it out and then opened an app.

"What are you doing?" he asked.

"Getting my magnifying app. I think I might see something...." She used her phone to magnify a part of the photo, then gasped. "I see it. I can see a person!"

"What? How?" Oliver asked.

"In the pupil of her eyes. There's a reflection of the person taking the photo."

"Let me see," Oliver said.

She showed him, and he let out a light gasp. "I know who that is."

She nodded. "I do, too. And it's terrifying me. Show me the old picture again, the one from ten years ago."

He pulled it out of his pocket, and she used the magnifying app again, then let out a small shriek. "It's the same person."

A branch snapped, the sound sharp and deliberate in the quietude of the surrounding forest. Instantly, Lisa's heart leaped into her throat, her phone slipping from numb fingers as she locked eyes with Oliver. Fear flickered there, a reflection of her own alarm.

"Did you hear that?" she hissed, her ears straining for more sounds, her body tensing for flight or fight.

Oliver nodded, silent, his protective instincts flaring to life as he moved toward the window, peering into the encroaching dusk. There was no mistaking the feeling that washed over them—the oppressive sense that the mountain held more than just echoes of the past—it may also harbor the eyes of the present, watching and waiting.

"Let's not jump to conclusions," he murmured, though his posture spoke of readiness—of a man who would face whatever threat loomed just beyond their makeshift sanctuary.

Lisa took both photos and put them in her pocket. These puzzle pieces were too precious to leave behind, keys to unlocking the web of secrets that entangled Michelle's disappearance. With one last glance around the cabin, a haven of clues now turned precarious, they steeled themselves for what lay beyond the wooden walls.

Together, they edged toward the back door, the thrill of the hunt now overshadowed by the chilling realization that in seeking the truth, they may have exposed themselves to dangers untold.

The crunch of boots on forest litter seemed unnaturally loud as Lisa and Oliver, laden with the weight of discovery, moved swiftly away from the cabin, leaving out the backdoor. Each rustling leaf and snapping twig sent shivers down Lisa's spine, a constant reminder that they might not be alone in the impenetrable woods that cloaked the mountainside.

"Keep going," Oliver whispered, his voice barely audible above the pounding of their hearts and the rush of the wind through the trees. Their hands clasped tightly were an unspoken pact of protection and solidarity. The evidence inside Lisa's jeans pocket felt like both a treasure and a target, the Polaroid pictures a mosaic of Michelle's lost years.

They emerged into the clearing where their truck waited like a loyal steed, moonlight glinting off its hood. The familiar sight was a balm to their jangled nerves. They wasted no time climbing inside, the door thuds echoing finality and urgency.

The engine roared to life as Oliver turned the key in the ignition, punctuating their escape. They drove in silence, the only sounds being gravel crunching beneath tires and the rapid breathing that filled the vehicle's cabin. In the passenger seat, Lisa's mind raced as fast as they were retreating, piecing together the new information with the old.

The warm glow of streetlights welcomed them back to civilization, and for a moment, Lisa allowed herself to relax. But the thread of unease remained, tugging at her conscience. She glanced over at Oliver, noting the set of his jaw, the way his hands gripped the steering wheel—signals of a resolve tempered by fear.

"Thank you for coming with me today," she said softly, breaking the silence. Her words were more than gratitude; they were an acknowledgment of their shared journey, both physical and emotional.

Oliver gave her a tight smile that didn't quite reach his eyes, which were still shadowed with thoughts of what might lurk in the mountains. "This was important to me."

As they pulled up to Maggie's house, the comforting sight of the cozy dwelling offered a promise of safety and normalcy. Yet, Lisa's heart ached with the knowledge that she could not fully share in this refuge. Trust was a fortress she'd built around her children, and though Oliver's sobriety was a beacon of hope, it was also a fragile flame easily extinguished by the winds of past demons.

"Are you sure you won't come home?" Oliver asked, his voice laced with concern and the faintest trace of hurt.

Lisa reached over, squeezing his hand and finding strength in the touch. "I need to be with the kids tonight. And Maggie... she understands. We'll figure this out together, I promise. Small steps."

He nodded, accepting her decision, recognizing the silent battles she fought within the walls of her heart. They parted with a lingering look that spoke volumes— their connection transcending words, the quest for truth binding them tighter than ever.

Inside, the laughter and warmth of family enveloped Lisa as she embraced Ethan, Abigail, Julia, and Daniel. Their innocent faces were a reminder of all that was at stake. Maggie welcomed her with open arms, a steady rock in the turbulent sea of uncertainty.

"Everything okay?" Maggie asked, her eyes searching Lisa's.

"Getting there," Lisa replied with a small, hopeful smile. "We're getting there."

With the children tucked in bed and the house quiet around them, Lisa sat at the kitchen table with Maggie, poring over the evidence once again, each clue a step closer to unraveling the mystery. Outside, the night held its breath, and inside, two women stood guard over a family, ready to face whatever the dawn might bring.

Chapter Nine

The computer screen's glow cast a pale light on Lisa Thompson's focused expression as she clicked through digitized archives, her eyes scanning the faded print of decade-old newspapers. The quiet hum of the laptop fan was a gentle accompaniment to the rhythmic tapping of her fingers on the keyboard, the only sounds in the room save for the occasional distant laughter of her children playing outside.

She leaned closer, her brown hair falling like a curtain around her face, isolating her from everything but the task at hand. A search term caught her eye, and she paused, heart pounding with hope and trepidation.

Lisa's breath hitched; this could be the breakthrough she needed. She printed the article, barely glancing at the paper as it slid out from the printer, her mind already racing ahead. She couldn't sit idle, not when there were answers out there begging to be uncovered. She still lived at Maggie's and had been there for three weeks now. She wasn't ready to go back, even though Oliver showed no signs of drinking. Past mistakes with her abusive ex-husband had taught her to be careful not to get pulled back, at least not too soon. She was nervous to go back, worried it would all return to the same, and she couldn't let that happen.

With a quickness born of urgency, she jotted down notes on a nearby pad, underlining names and dates with a determined stroke.

The article mentioned a quaint town just a few hours' drive away. The decision was made. Lisa stood up, and her movements were decisive. She grabbed her coat, slipped into its familiar warmth, and found Maggie in the living room.

"Could you look after them for a while?" she asked.

"No problem," Maggie said with a wink. "Go do whatever you need to."

Her car engine came to life with a comforting rumble, and Lisa navigated down the winding roads that led away from their small Alaskan town. The scenery was a blur as she drove, her thoughts instead on the woman she'd never met but felt a connection to all the same—Oliver's sister.

Lisa's pulse quickened as the town's welcome sign came into view, a flutter of excitement mingling with the persistent ache of fear. What if she was being led on a wild goose chase? Or worse, what if she found what she was looking for?

She parked on the main street, the quiet bustle of

the small town enveloping her. This place held secrets, and Lisa was determined to coax them into the light.

"Can I help you, ma'am?" a passerby asked, noticing the out-of-towner looking lost in thought.

"Perhaps," Lisa said with a smile that belied her nerves. "I'm looking for anyone who might remember seeing a woman about ten years ago. She may have passed through here."

The local nodded, a flicker of recognition crossing their features. "You should talk to old Mrs. Hanson. She has a memory like a steel trap. Runs the bar just over on Elm Street."

"Thank you," Lisa said, her gratitude genuine. This was it, the next step. As she walked toward Elm Street, her strides were strong and purposeful. She was a woman on a mission, fueled by love and fortified by resolve. Oliver's sister's story was waiting to be told, and Lisa would be the one to tell it.

The bell above the door chimed softly as Lisa stepped into the dimly lit bar, a stark contrast to the crisp autumn air that had followed her in. The scent of aged wood and spilled beer was oddly comforting, grounding her as she scanned the room for someone who might hold a piece of the past.

"Evening," she greeted the bartender, a woman with streaks of gray in her hair and an easy smile that reached her eyes. Mrs. Hanson, she guessed. "I was wondering if you could help me with something."

The bartender dried her hands on a towel and leaned closer, interest piqued. "What can I do for ya?"

"I'm looking for information about a woman who might have been here about ten years ago." Lisa slid a worn photo across the bar, the edges frayed from time and handling. "She looked like this."

It was a long shot, but she had to try. If Michelle had been here, then it would add another piece to the puzzle.

The bartender studied the picture, a slow nod shaping her response. "Yeah, I remember her. Came in here quite a bit. Always sat in that corner booth, by herself mostly." She gestured toward the back of the room, where a solitary booth seemed to absorb the shadows.

"Did she ever talk to anyone? Did she seem... troubled to you?" Lisa's voice was soft but insistent, her hazel eyes searching for any flicker of memory that might surface.

"Troubled, yeah, I'd say so," the bartender replied, her expression turning thoughtful. "Quiet, kept to herself. There were whispers, you know, that she had her share of demons. But she never caused any trouble here."

"When was the last time you saw her?" she asked. "Do you recall?"

She looked pensive. "As a matter of fact, I do. It was a couple of months ago, in August, I believe. She came in looking a little distressed. I asked her if she was all right, and she said she was, and to just give her the usual. But then, someone came in and sat with her. That's why I remembered it. Yes, someone was here with her for the first time—a guy."

With her heart throbbing in her throat, Lisa pulled out a picture taken from his Facebook profile—the same guy who had been in the Polaroid photos.

"Could it have been this guy?"

Mrs. Hanson looked at it and nodded. "Yup. That's him. There's no doubt about it. I'd recognize that face anywhere."

"Thank you," Lisa murmured, her heart pounding a rhythm of hope and trepidation. She moved toward the corner booth, feeling the weight of countless stories that lingered like ghosts among the stale air and scratched wood.

Sliding onto the worn seat, Lisa turned her attention to the patrons around her. The regulars continued their conversations, laughter erupting occasionally like the crackling of a fire against the silence. She recognized the type: hardy souls with weathered faces, each with a tale etched into the lines of their skin.

"Mind if I join you?" Lisa asked an older man whose eyes held the depth of the ocean, his face carved from years at sea.

He glanced up, curiosity winning over reluctance. "Sure thing, miss. What brings you to our little corner of the world?"

Lisa explained, her voice threaded with resolve,

how she was searching for answers about her sister-in-law, trying to piece together a life that had unraveled in silence and shadow. The man listened, nodding along, his gaze never leaving her face.

"Ah, yes, I remember her," he said finally. "She had a look about her—like she was waiting for something or running from it. Never could tell which."

"Did she meet anyone here? Friends, maybe?" Lisa pressed, her instincts on high alert.

"Friends?" he scoffed gently, shaking his head. "No, but there were people looking for her now and then. They came down by the docks and asked questions. I can't say they were friends, though."

"Looking for her?" Lisa echoed, her pulse quickening.

"Yep, some guy asking questions, same as you're doing. Didn't seem too friendly, if you catch my drift." His eyes held a cautionary glint.

"Was it this guy?" she asked, showing him the same printed-out photo she had shown Mrs. Hanson.

"Well, yes, that's him. Didn't like him much. Never told him about the girl or the child."

"What do you mean *the child*?" she asked.

"She had a kid. Young one at the time; he's about nine now."

"Where is he?" she asked, startled.

"Lives with his dad, Jonas Hesston. They had a house a little out of town."

"Do you know the address?" Lisa asked, her heart

racing hard in her chest. Michelle had a son? Oliver had a nephew? This changed everything.

"Sure, I'll write it on a napkin," he said. "Hey, Edna, do you have a pen?"

Mrs. Hanson brought one to him, and he wrote an address on a white napkin. "Here you go. Nice fella. He should be friendly to you."

"Thank you," Lisa said, offering a warm, appreciative smile that masked the cold dread creeping up her spine. "You've been very helpful."

As she left the bar, the puzzle pieces began to form a clearer image, one that promised answers yet hinted at danger lurking beneath the surface. Her determination solidified; she would not be deterred. For Oliver, for his sister, for justice, Lisa would chase down every lead, no matter where it took her. The thrill of the hunt surged within her, propelling her forward into the unknown.

The journey back to her own small town was a blur, the landscape a monochrome smear beyond the car window. Lisa gripped the wheel, her knuckles white, each mile bringing her closer to a confrontation she never imagined having with Oliver.

When she reached the outskirts of town, twilight had cast its indigo hue over the world, and the Thompson family café came into view like an oasis of warmth. She parked and sat for a moment, gathering the shattered pieces of her resolve.

"Oliver needs to know," she murmured to herself. "He deserves the truth."

She found him in the back amidst a graveyard of wood shavings and half-finished projects, his hands moving with a craftsman's grace over a piece of cedar. He looked up, his smile fading at the sight of her solemn expression.

"Lisa? What's wrong?"

She approached, the distance between them charged with unspoken truths. Her hands shook as she told him everything she had learned today.

For a long moment, Oliver said nothing, the silence stretching taut between them. Then, his shoulders slumped, defeat and sorrow etching deep lines across his brow.

"Let's sit down," he whispered.

They moved to the small table they used for impromptu family dinners, the wood scarred with memories. There, under the dim light of a single bulb, Oliver nodded slowly, letting it all sink in.

"I have a nephew?"

Lisa swallowed and placed a hand on top of his. "Yes. He lives with his dad. According to the locals, Michelle left one day and never came back. The dad assumed she had taken off—leaving him and the kid. That's how the story went. So, he's been taking care of him for the past six months, probably not knowing what happened to her since no one knew where she had been or where she lived—or even that she had a family."

"Wow."

She exhaled. "I know. It's a lot for one day."

Oliver met her gaze, and she saw the reflection of their shared resolve in his eyes.

"Thank you, Lisa," he said, his voice thick with unshed tears. "For not giving up."

"Never," she vowed, the word a solemn pledge that bound them together in the heart-pounding pursuit of truth.

Oliver's hands trembled as he clasped them tightly on the kitchen table, the pale light casting shadows that seemed to deepen the worry lines etched across his face. The silence that hung between them was heavy, laden with the weight of impending revelations.

Lisa felt a chill trace its way up her spine, the sinister undercurrents of the small town suddenly breaking through the surface like jagged ice. She could sense Oliver's burden of guilt, a shroud that had draped over him since the tragedy.

"Oliver," she said softly, squeezing his hand in reassurance, "none of this is your fault. You did everything you could."

He looked up, his eyes haunted. "I should've protected her, Lisa. It was my job as her brother, and I failed. I can't believe she had a family?"

She knew no words could erase his self-reproach, but she needed him to understand that they had a chance to make things right. "We can still help her, Oliver. We can uncover the truth and bring those responsible to justice. You and I both don't believe she killed herself. Someone hurt her, and they're getting away with it."

Oliver glanced toward the liquor cabinet, and Lisa knew how badly he was craving a drink. All these wounds that had been opened threatened to drag him down into the darkness again. She grabbed his chin and pulled his head so he would look at her instead.

"I love you, Oliver. I love us. Forever and always."

It was then that a resolve settled over them both, solidifying their partnership in a quest for answers.

The sound of a knock at the door broke through their intense focus. Lisa rose to answer it, finding their neighbor Lyle standing on the porch, his stance unsteady and his gaze clouded with drink. She hadn't seen him since he tried to kiss her and she told him not to, that she was with Oliver and loved him despite his ex coming to town and wanting him back.

"Lisa," he slurred, his voice tinged with an edge of desperation, "let's leave all this behind. You and me, we could—"

But Lisa cut him off, placing a gentle yet firm hand on his chest. "Lyle, you know I can't do that. Oliver needs me now more than ever."

"Oliver?" Lyle scoffed, bitterness lacing his tone.

"He's a drunk, and he treats you like dirt. Why do you defend him?"

"Because he's more than his mistakes," Lisa insisted, her eyes blazing with conviction. "He's fighting his demons, and he needs someone to stand by him."

Anger flared in Lyle's eyes, and he shoved her hand away. "You're a fool, Lisa," he spat out before stumbling off into the cold night.

Closing the door on Lyle's retreating figure, Lisa leaned against the wood, taking a moment to steady her racing heart. Returning to Oliver, she found him waiting, his expression one of gratitude and silent understanding. He no longer looked like he craved a drink—only her love.

"Let's keep going," she said. "Let's figure this puzzle out together and get closure for you and your family."

The cold draft from the half-open window did little to deter Lisa's focus as she dialed Travis's number, her fingers tapping rhythmically on the kitchen table. Oliver stood by her side, his presence a solid comfort in the uncertain quest they were about to undertake. The phone rang twice before a gravelly voice answered.

"Travis speaking."

"Travis, it's Lisa Thompson," she said quickly, exchanging a glance with Oliver. "We need your help."

A brief pause followed, then a sigh that spoke of years spent in service and retirement that was anything but restful. "I figured this call might come sooner or later. What have you two found?"

Lisa briefed the retired officer on their discoveries, her words painting a picture of a decade-old mystery resurfacing like a ghost from the murky depths. Oliver interjected with details only he knew—the pain of loss giving weight to every fact shared.

"All right," Travis finally said, determination seeping through the line. "Let's meet. And bring every-thing you've got."

The three of them convened at the dimly lit back room of Lisa and Oliver's café, where the walls brimmed with the rich aroma of coffee beans and old wood. Travis, with his hawk-like gaze and silvered hair, listened intently as they laid out the information—printed-out newspaper clippings that led her to the town where Michelle had lived, the Polaroid photos of Michelle, the notes Lisa had taken when speaking to the locals in the town.

"First things first," Travis began, pulling out his notebook. We'll need to call in some favors. I've got contacts still in the force. If we play our cards right, they can get us access to databases."

Oliver nodded, his face set in grim resolve, while Lisa felt the flicker of hope ignite within her chest. They were no longer alone in this; they had an ally with knowledge and connections they sorely lacked.

The following weeks were a blur of activity. The trio worked tirelessly, following up on Travis's insights —staking out locations, piecing together timelines, and cross-referencing faces. Lisa learned to read the tension in Oliver's shoulders, offering support without words when the shadows of doubt crept in.

But with every clue uncovered, the air around them seemed to grow colder, charged with the unseen presence of a watcher. Lisa would double-check the locks on their doors at night, her dreams filled with dark alleys and whispers just beyond hearing. The thrill of the chase was marred by the chilling realization that the predator could turn on them at any moment.

"Stay vigilant," Travis would remind them. "These types are like cornered animals—they'll lash out when least expected."

And so, amidst heartwarming moments shared over cups of hot coffee and quiet evenings where Lisa and Oliver's hands would find each other's, there remained the electric hum of suspense. The thrill of being so close to truth mingled with the fear of what that truth might bring.

Yet through it all, Lisa held onto the love that bound her to Oliver, their family, and the memory of the woman whose life had been cut tragically short. It was this love that fueled their search, pushing them forward into the unknown, hearts racing with the promise of justice—a justice that had eluded Oliver's sister for far too long.

Chapter Ten

Lisa took a deep breath, her hazel eyes scanning the small, cluttered bedroom that once belonged to Oliver's late sister. This was where she had been for all those years, living here with her family. The air felt thick with dust and the heavy scent of old books, but beneath that, there was something else—a trace of mystery that clung to the corners like cobwebs. This place was a crypt of secrets, and she couldn't shake the feeling that one of them held the key to what really happened.

"She just left one day," Jonas, the father of her child, said. "I... I didn't know why. I kept thinking she might come back. But her suitcase was gone along with some of her clothes. I assumed she had left me and Sammy. I couldn't never have imagined...."

Jonas trailed off. He was standing in the doorway to the bedroom. Oliver and Lisa had asked nicely if they could go through Michelle's things after telling him what they believed had happened to her. He didn't even know she was dead, he said. It had knocked the air out of him, and he had just been sitting there for a long time on the couch downstairs while they waited for him to gather his thoughts. He was just now able to talk. Lisa didn't know what she was looking for, but there had to be something they could use, something that could direct them toward Michelle's whereabouts in the days before her death.

Her fingers trailed over the desktop, pushing aside stacks of paper in search of anything out of place. The official police report had been clear: an unfortunate suicide, a case closed as quickly as it had opened. However, Lisa's heart, a vessel tempered by past violence and loss, refused to accept such a tidy conclusion. There were shadows here that didn't match the light, whispers in the silence that spoke of hidden truths. A person had been with her in that cabin, taking photos of her. The same person who stood behind her ten years ago before she left without a word. This person could have been with her when she died. But how could they prove it?

A photo frame, face down, caught her attention. She picked it up, swiping away the layer of grime to reveal a smiling family that no longer existed. It was a snapshot of happier times—before grief carved its hollows into Oliver's strong yet introspective features.

"Where are you leading me?" she murmured to the

absent girl in the photograph, her voice a blend of warmth and resolve.

The walls seemed to press closer, listening as Lisa continued her search. She was methodical, knowing that any misstep could crumble the path she was forging toward the truth. Each drawer she opened and every piece of paper she sifted through brought a mix of hope and anxiety. The excitement of the chase was there, the thrill of uncovering what was meant to stay buried. Yet, the suspense gnawed at her bones, the fear of what she might find—or what might find her—never quite leaving her side.

In a bottom drawer, hidden beneath a stack of old magazines, Lisa discovered a collection of receipts, each meticulously filed by date. They spanned back months before that fateful day, and as she examined them, she noted purchases that made little sense for a woman supposedly preparing to end her own life. A new coat? Hiking boots? A new computer? The items spoke of plans, of futures being envisioned.

"Oliver," she whispered. His pain was hers now, and his sister's enigmatic end was a puzzle they both needed to solve—not just for peace but for protection—for their family that had been built on resilience and the tender bonds of stepchildren who called him dad.

Lisa tucked the receipts into her bag, her pulse quickening. There was more to this story; she could feel it in her bones. And she wouldn't stop until the whole town knew it, too.

Lisa's fingertips traced the spines of books inside the dusty box, the musty smell of old paper and forgotten memories hanging heavy in the air of Oliver's child-hood home. The box in the attic contained a few of Michelle's things she left behind that their parents thought they'd keep. Oliver had brought it down to his old room, and they were going through it together. Lisa paused at a book that had no writing on the back.

With a gentle tug, the book came loose, heavier than its counterparts. A hollow echo sounded as it left its resting place. Heart pounding with the thrill of potential discovery, Lisa peered into the gap the book had left, catching the faintest glint of metal in the shadows.

"Come on," she whispered, reaching down. Her fingers wrapped around a small key, cool to the touch and embossed with intricate filigree that suggested importance and secrecy. It took only a moment to find the lock it fit, camouflaged in the wall paneling in Michelle's old room. With a soft click, a hidden drawer edged open, revealing its clandestine treasure: a diary bound in leather that whispered of mysteries held tight for far too long.

Lisa's breath hitched as she lifted the journal, an inexplicable sense of connection passing through her. This was no ordinary diary; it was a silent witness to Michelle's life and perhaps her final days before she left. This could hold the answers as to the why. Why did she leave?

Lisa hesitated, knowing that the pages within might hold answers for which she wasn't prepared. But the love she bore for Oliver and the need to protect the patchwork family they had woven together steeled her resolve.

The entries were cryptic, a code of half-sentences and veiled references that spoke of fear and urgency. Dates were circled with frenzied pen strokes, names mentioned alongside question marks, and ominous doodles filled the margins like dark clouds threatening a storm.

"Your sister was scared," Lisa told Oliver, the realization dawning like an unwelcome sunrise. "She must have been running from something or someone."

As Lisa turned the pages, soaking in the fragmented thoughts and fears penned down in a rushed hand, the official story of a young woman overwhelmed by despair began to crumble. They had found receipts that indicated plans for the future, purchases made with hope found in her home, along with a family that loved her and a child who needed her—none of it aligned with the image of someone at the brink of self-destruction.

"Someone else was definitely involved," Lisa concluded, a shiver of suspense running down her spine. The entries hinted at meetings in hushed tones and the palpable sense of being in great danger. Every word written was a piece of the puzzle, gradually forming a picture that Oliver's sister had been ensnared in a web much larger than anyone had imagined.

Lisa clutched the diary to her chest, its secrets now entrusted to her care. She knew she was treading on dangerous ground, unraveling a truth that had been buried under layers of silence and deceit. Yet, for Oliver, for their children, for the memory of a woman who had seemingly run out of options, she would face the unknown.

Lisa's fingers grasped the doorknob, the cold metal biting into her skin as she returned to Maggie's house. Oliver had dropped her off, and Maggie had taken the kids out for dinner, so she was all alone. She stood in the kitchen, thinking of all she had discovered these past few days and weeks. It had changed her view of the world —a world that now felt infinitely more treacherous than ever before. She paused, taking a deep breath to steady her racing heart.

She sat down with a cup of tea, trying to settle her anxiety and worry, which had grown increasingly intense lately. She was scrolling on her phone when a soft rustle from outside the back door to the kitchen pierced the stillness, slicing through the silence like a warning shot.

Lisa stilled, every muscle tensing, her instincts flaring to life. The noise was distinct—the crunch of dry leaves under cautious footsteps, deliberate and measured. Her mind raced, cataloging every possibility. Could it be a wildlife creature? Or was it something far more sinister?

The comforting weight of the diary on the table served as a silent reminder of what was at stake. She knew she couldn't allow fear to paralyze her—not when Oliver's sister's story hung in the balance, begging to be told. But caution was paramount; she could not afford recklessness with so much on the line.

Without making a sound, Lisa gently checked that the door was locked. The shadows in the corners of the room seemed to grow longer and thicker, swallowing up the fading light and casting an eerie gloom over the wooden interior.

Her breath, ragged and shallow, was the only sound in the heavy silence that enveloped her. She strained her ears, searching for another hint of movement, but there was nothing—only the deafening quiet that mocked her anxiety.

Seconds stretched into minutes as Lisa debated her next move. Should she reveal herself or wait out the potential threat? The decision weighed heavily upon her, burdened by the unknown face of danger lurking just beyond the walls.

Then, without warning, the floorboards groaned softly near the window. Lisa's heart lurched into her throat, adrenaline surging through her veins. Her gaze snapped to the source of the sound, eyes wide with alarm.

Silhouetted against the dimming light outside, she

saw it—a shadow, distorted and vague but unmistakably human. It shifted, pausing as if sensing her awareness, then continued its stealthy advance.

Lisa's resolve hardened into steel. She backed away from the door, her hand finding the cool surface of a table for support, wondering who this mysterious figure was.

Chapter Eleven

The kitchen's silence shattered as a dark shadow lunged at Lisa from the corner. Her heart hammered against her ribs, a primal fear igniting every nerve in her body. There was no time to scream—only to react. Muscle memory kicked in; the countless hours she had invested in self-defense after her tumultuous past with her abusive ex-husband now fueled her every move.

Lisa's foot shot out, connecting with a thud against the assailant's knee. A grunt of pain emanated from the figure, but they remained relentless, their hands clawing at her with desperate strength. She twisted her torso, evading a crushing grip, and her elbow swung back hard into what she hoped was the attacker's face. The shadow staggered momentarily, giving her a precious second.

"Think, Lisa, think," she whispered, her mind racing as fast as her heart. She remembered the pepper spray Oliver had insisted she keep in her purse—the purse that lay far away on the rustic coffee table—not an option now.

Her assailant recovered, reaching for her again with a ferocity that chilled her blood. However, Lisa was no stranger to survival; adversity had been her unwanted companion for years, and it had taught her well. Her palm struck the shadow's nose with a forceful jab.

A burst of adrenaline surged through her veins, a tidal wave of energy that seemed to come from the very depths of her soul. It was the same indefatigable spirit that had helped her protect her children, run a business, and face life's cruelties head-on.

In that moment of frenetic struggle, she found a gap in her attacker's guard. With all her might, she pushed against the oppressive weight, her body screaming in protest. And then, like breaking through ice into the air above, she was free.

She pivoted on her heel, heart pounding a frantic rhythm that matched her sprint. Her focus was singular —escape. But as momentum carried her forward, a rug slipped beneath her feet, sending her sprawling to the wooden floor.

"Get up, Lisa. For Ethan, Abigail, Julia... for Daniel," she murmured, invoking her children's names like a talisman against the darkness. With grit and resolve, she clambered to her feet, barely noticing the bruises that would later bloom like unwelcome flowers on her skin.

The back door beckoned in the distance, a beacon

of safety in the night. Yet even as she fled toward it, she knew this was far from over. Whoever had attacked her in this once-safe haven was connected to the secrets she was unearthing—secrets someone was willing to protect at any cost.

However, Lisa Thompson was not a woman who cowered in the shadows. She was a mother, a fighter, and a survivor. And nothing would stop her from bringing the truth to light.

Lisa's breaths tore from her lungs as she dashed across the room, a maelstrom of dread and determination swirling within her. The metallic taste of fear lingered on her tongue, but her heart's relentless pounding filled her ears, amplifying with each stride toward the door that promised freedom. Her hands, slick with perspiration, betrayed her as they fumbled over the cold, unforgiving brass of the lock. She cursed silently, urging her trembling fingers to work faster.

"Come on," she whispered, a prayer escaping her lips. With a click that resonated like a gunshot in the silence, the lock yielded. The door swung open with a groan, spilling the chill of the night and the scent of pine into the kitchen. Without a second glance, Lisa burst out into the obsidian embrace of the darkness that soon enveloped her like a cloak.

Her feet found the rhythm instinctively, crunching over the frosted ground as she propelled herself forward. The sounds of the forest were both ally and adversary—masking her escape yet reminding her she wasn't alone. Lisa knew this terrain; it had been a silent spectator to many of her family excursions, a haven before it became a hunting ground. But tonight, under the cloak of fear, every shadow seemed menacing, every rustle a herald of danger.

A sudden snap of twigs behind her sent a shard of panic through her spine. The pursuer was close, too close. Her legs pumped harder, her breaths now jagged blades cutting through the frigid air. She imagined her children's faces, eyes wide with trust, innocent to the horrors that lurked beyond their cozy café and warm beds. It was for them she ran, and for them, she would never stop.

"Oliver...."

His name came unbidden, a balm to her soul. Would he forgive her if she didn't make it back? A sob caught in her throat, but she stifled it, converting the surge of emotion into energy, fueling her flight.

The trees blurred past as Lisa pushed herself, willing her muscles to obey despite their protests. Every step was a defiance, every gasp a declaration. She was Lisa Thompson—mother, wife, survivor—and she would not be hunted. Not tonight, not ever. As the chilling breeze lashed against her face, mixing with the tears that had begun to fall, she felt a spark ignite within her. She was more than her fear; she was fire and fight woven into flesh.

The silver glint of the car's metal under the moonlight in the driveway outside Maggie's house was a siren call to safety. Lisa ran through the backyard and out into the street to get around the house. Lisa's sprint was desperate, her boots pounding against the gravel as if she could outrun her own shadow. The keychain jingled in her grasp, a discordant symphony to her ragged breaths. She reached the car, her trembling fingers betraying her as they struggled to select the right key.

"Come on; come on," she whispered, a prayer to the midnight stillness.

Her heart lurched as a rough hand tangled in her hair, yanking her back with a violence that stole the air from her lungs. Terror and rage intertwined, sparking a fierce defiance within her. Twisting around, Lisa's survival instinct took over. She thrust the key forward, and it found its mark in the assailant's shoulder.

A guttural groan pierced the night, and Lisa seized the moment. Her key plunged into the lock, turning with an audible click, and she threw herself inside the sanctuary of her vehicle. Slamming the door shut, she locked it just as quickly, her hands now slick with sweat and something warmer, stickier.

Blood. Her assailant's blood.

Breathing hard, Lisa jammed the key into the ignition, the engine roaring to life beneath her. The headlights cut through the darkness, revealing nothing but the deserted path ahead. She didn't hesitate, foot slamming down on the accelerator, the tires spinning before catching on the dirt road and propelling her forward.

As Maggie's house receded into the night, like a nightmare fading at the break of dawn, Lisa forced herself to glance in the rearview mirror. No silhouettes gave chase; no footsteps echoed after her. Only the winding road stretched behind, empty and silent.

"Safe," she gasped, allowing the word to fill the cramped space of the car, a tentative balm to her frayed nerves.

Yet, as relief mingled with the adrenaline coursing through her veins, a part of her ached with the knowledge of who had lurked in the shadows. That face that had been obscured by the dark yet recognizable to her and those rough hands that sought to harm her.

The very thought was terrifying.

Lisa knew one thing for sure: the threads of this story were far from unraveled, and she would follow them wherever they led. For now, though, she focused on the road unwinding before her, each mile a step back to the life she fought so fiercely to protect.

Lisa's grip on the steering wheel was white-knuckled, and the engine's hum was a steady companion to the erratic beat of her heart. She sped along the moonlit road that cut through town, her thoughts careening as wildly as her vehicle. The chilling encounter at

Maggie's house had left her with more than just the sting where she'd been grabbed.

"I'm not letting you get away with this," she whispered into the void, the statement meant for the shadowy figure who had attacked her. It was the same statement she'd made to herself countless times about the circumstances shrouding Michelle's untimely death. This person wanted to intimidate her, to keep her from digging too deep, from unearthing secrets best left buried in the frozen ground.

Her headlights threw long shadows across the road, and in the brief moments when fear subsided, Lisa allowed herself to think of what had brought her here— of Oliver's sister, a woman whose laughter once filled the rooms of his childhood home, now silenced. The recollection tightened around her chest like a vise. She remembered his accounts of the silent meals at the house after she left, the looks exchanged that were heavy with things unspoken.

Oliver's sister had struggled against currents both seen and unseen, battling demons that Lisa had only glimpsed. She'd fought for love in a place where it seemed in short supply, reaching out for connections that repeatedly slipped through her fingers like fine sand. And then, one day, she had vanished, leaving behind an aching void that echoed with the questions no one dared to voice.

"It all comes down to Sammy..." Lisa pondered aloud.

The thought sent a cold shiver down her spine,

merging seamlessly with the chill of the night air that seeped through the car's vents. The truth was out there, somewhere beneath the layers of silence and snow, and Lisa felt it calling to her—a siren song that promised answers but also warned of peril.

But who would believe her?

She blinked away the beginnings of tears, not of fear but of frustration. Oliver's sister deserved justice; her story begged to be told, and Lisa would be the one to tell it, no matter the cost. Her resolve hardened, becoming impenetrable as the permafrost holding this town in its icy grip.

"Whatever secrets you're hiding," Lisa murmured, eyes fixed on the road ahead, "I will find them. I will get you."

And with each mile she put between herself and the house, her determination grew, fueled by the knowledge that the key to unlocking the past lay within her grasp. The fight at the house had shown her the depth of her own strength, the fierceness of a mother and wife who would stop at nothing to protect her family, honor a memory, and bring a hidden truth into the light.

With her hands tight on the wheel, Lisa's thoughts whirled like a snowstorm in her mind. She could almost feel Oliver's sister beside her, a ghostly presence filled with anguish and secrets. The pain of being misunderstood, the burden of family strife, and the final, crushing despair that must have enveloped her before she vanished all resonated within Lisa's heart, drawing out a profound empathy for the woman she'd never met.

"Oliver," she whispered to the emptiness, "I'll prove to the world what happened to her. I promise."

Her voice wavered, not from doubt but from an overwhelming sense of purpose. It wasn't just about solving a mystery; it was about honoring a life cut short and about bringing peace to those left behind.

A shiver ran down her spine as she considered the implications. The assailant had been real, flesh and blood, driven by motives dark enough to attack her. This person was dangerous and wouldn't stop until she was silenced. But fear wouldn't deter her. For Oliver, for justice, and for closure, she couldn't let the specter of danger extinguish her quest.

Her eyes caught a glint on the dashboard: the keys that had pierced her attacker's shoulder. They now symbolized more than just her escape; they were a testament to her resolve. She gripped them briefly, feeling their cold metal against her skin before letting them go again.

"Okay, Lisa, focus," she murmured, steering her thoughts back to the task at hand. The roads may be deserted, the evening silent except for the thrum of the car's engine, but she wasn't alone in this. She carried her family's strength, her husband's love, and the resilience that life had hammered into her soul.

Her gaze flickered to the rearview mirror, half expecting to see headlights tailing her, but there were none. Only shadows chased her now—shadows of doubt and fear that she swiftly banished with the thought of her children.

She grabbed her phone, called Maggie, and told her what had happened. She then told Maggie to meet her at the café with the children. They'd have to spend the night there tonight.

"No one is going to hurt my family," she declared, her voice steady and sure. The road stretched ahead, winding through the darkness, a metaphor for the journey she was on. Uncovering the truth would be treacherous, possibly even deadly, but she'd walk through fire before she let the unknown threaten her loved ones.

As the miles passed, Lisa allowed herself a moment of vulnerability, the night's events catching up with her. Her chest tightened, not with panic, but with the fierce love of a mother bear protecting her cubs.

"Justice will be served," she vowed, her words a silent oath to the stillness of the Alaskan night. And with each turn of the wheels, her determination became a beacon, piercing through the veil of fear and uncertainty, guiding her inexorably toward the truth that lay hidden within the heart of their small town.

She then called Oliver and said with tears in her voice, "We're coming home."

Chapter Twelve

The chime of the cell phone cut through the hum of the café like a sharp knife, pulling Lisa from her thoughts. She wiped her hands on her apron as she glanced at the screen, expecting nothing more than the usual business-related message or a text from one of the kids. Instead, the words that met her eyes were stark and unadorned, yet they sent a shiver down her spine.

"I got something. Meet?"

Her heart pounded against her ribcage, a staccato rhythm that matched the buzz of fear and anticipation coursing through her veins. Lisa slipped into the back office, ensuring privacy, before typing a cautious reply.

"When?" she responded.

For a moment, Lisa considered the risk. The last thing she wanted was to dredge up past horrors or place her family in danger's path again. It had been two weeks since the attack, but she was still marked by it and didn't sleep well at night.

Lisa took a deep breath, her eyes darkening with resolve. It was a dance with shadows, but she was no stranger to the darkness. With a sense of purpose steadying her shaky hands, she composed another message, designating a location she knew well—the old mill by the river, secluded enough to ensure confidentiality yet familiar enough for her to control the setting.

"Tomorrow. Sunrise. Old Mill," she wrote, her thumb hesitating for a heartbeat before hitting send.

There was no turning back now. She locked her phone and tucked it into the pocket of her jeans, feeling its weight against her thigh like a talisman. Lisa emerged from the office with her usual warm smile, though it didn't quite reach her eyes. She moved through the motions of clearing tables and serving customers, the matriarch of this community hub she had built with Oliver. No one could know the turmoil that churned beneath her calm exterior.

As closing time neared, Lisa shared a tender glance with Oliver, his dark hair flecked with sawdust, a testament to his day's labor. His strong hands, always so gentle with her and the kids, gave her silent strength. He nodded subtly, sensing her unease, his protective nature a silent vow between them. After the attack at Maggie's house, he had told her they needed to take a step back. It was getting too dangerous. He didn't want his family to have to live in fear. They were done. Let it go, he said. But Lisa still couldn't. She refused to.

"Everything okay?" he mouthed across the room, his

concern evident even amidst the clatter of dishes and the fading chatter.

Lisa nodded reassuringly, not wanting to burden him with her fears just yet. "Soon," she thought, "when I have something concrete to share."

That night, after tucking the children into bed and sharing a quiet dinner with Oliver, Lisa lay awake, staring at the ceiling. Her mind replayed the possible scenarios of the upcoming meeting and whether or not it would be dangerous. Yet, within her chest, a fire burned—a fire fueled by love and determination. For her family, for Oliver, for the justice Michelle deserved, she would face the unknown. Oliver would have to understand. She couldn't tell him about it yet; he would only try and stop her from going.

As dawn approached, cloaking the town in a veil of misty gray, Lisa set out toward the old mill, her senses heightened. The thrill of the chase pulsed through her, mingled with the warmth of the rising sun that promised a new day. Today might bring answers or more questions, but either way, Lisa Thompson would be ready.

The chill of the abandoned mill seeped into Lisa's bones as she waited, her breath forming small clouds in the cold morning air. She paced, the crunch of gravel underfoot breaking the eerie silence. Each step was a testament to her resolve, and when a figure finally emerged from the tree line, her heart skipped a beat.

"Detective Ramirez. Are you sure no one followed you here?" Lisa asked, her voice steady despite the adrenaline coursing through her veins.

Ramirez nodded. "I saw him... Sheriff Jim," he whispered, his voice laced with fear, "I've been following him for days since you told me he attacked you, and you saw him at the scene. He went back to the cabin where she was found. I took pictures, even though it means I could lose my job."

"That doesn't really prove anything," Lisa said. "We need something more solid. The Polaroid photos aren't quite enough. The old news stories, either. We all know he is the one who killed her, and he attacked me. But how do we prove it? How do we prove that Sheriff Jim Coleman murdered Michelle?"

Lisa's blood ran cold when she heard herself say the sheriff's name. She could still feel those fingers as they grabbed her hair and pulled. She could feel his breath on her skin, and all she could think about was that those eyes were the last thing poor Michelle had seen.

"Let me finish," Ramirez said. "There's more."

"Tell me everything," she urged, her eyes fixed intently on the figure before her.

"I found a witness."

Lisa's eyes grew wide. "A witness? To what?"

"A hunter. He was in the mountains when he heard the shot fired. He rushed toward the cabin to see what had happened and saw Sheriff Coleman leaving the cabin and rushing into his car. He then ran to look inside and saw Michelle. She was lying on the bed, a bullet wound to her head, the gun placed in her hand. He was the one who called the police and told them that someone was dead and where to find her."

"Why wasn't he mentioned in the report, then?" Lisa asked. "There was no witness statement. They only said it was called in anonymously."

"When I spoke to him, he said he was never questioned. The sheriff arrived with his deputies, and as soon as he saw them, he realized that it was the same guy, so he took off. He never got to tell his story. He didn't dare to. But I convinced him to tell me about it. I'm not sure he has the guts to tell it again, though. But it's something."

"And he is certain that it was him?" Lisa probed, seeking clarity amid the shocking revelation.

"Positive," Ramirez affirmed with a shudder. "He said he has never been more sure of anything in his life."

"Did the sheriff see him?" Lisa's mind raced with the implications of his testimony. "Could he be in danger?"

"No, I don't think so. He said he was careful."

"Okay, and so must we be. Not a word to anyone."

"Naturally. And remember, you didn't hear any of it from me. I don't want to lose my job."

As Detective Ramirez faded back into the woods, Lisa stood alone once more, the echo of their parting steps a stark reminder of the perilous path ahead. The sun rose on the horizon, casting long shadows across the derelict structure, a silent witness to the warmth and the chill of the truths unearthed. She couldn't shake the feeling that every step toward justice drew her further into the crosshairs of a deadly game. Yet, for Oliver, Michelle, and the son who might never know the truth, Lisa Thompson would not be deterred. She would chase this sinister truth to the very end, her love a shield against the darkness that threatened to consume her.

Lisa's fingers trembled as she held the phone with the digital recorder app open, its red light glowing like a beacon in the dim morning light. She replayed the last few seconds of Ramirez's testimony, ensuring every word had been captured—a lifeline in the storm that was surely coming. This way, if anything happened to him, she would be able to keep the evidence. With each harrowing detail preserved in the device's memory, she felt the weight of the truth and the burden of her next steps.

"Michelle's boy... he deserves to know," Lisa whispered to herself, her gaze hardening with resolve.

As she returned to her car, Lisa's mind raced with the implications of what she'd learned. Sheriff Jim—the fatherly figure who'd patted children's heads and led the town's Fourth of July parade—was a predator masked by his badge. The magnitude of his betrayal was unfathomable, yet here in her hands lay the fragile beginnings of his undoing.

Ensuring every piece of evidence was securely saved, Lisa made sure to save the recordings to her cloud. Her heart thudded against her ribs; every sound in the secluded clearing felt amplified, every rustle of leaves a potential alarm. She needed to move, to put distance between herself and this place before the world woke up to discover her meddling.

Like a shadow melting into the underbrush, Lisa took one last look around the clearing. She couldn't let fear take root; she thought of her children's faces and Oliver's unwavering trust and steeled herself for the road ahead.

She retraced her steps with practiced care, avoiding the patches of soft earth she'd memorized on her way in. Each footfall was placed with precision, leaving no trace of her passage. Her breaths came in controlled whispers, blending with the cool breeze that stirred the trees into hushed conversation.

Pausing at the edge of the woods, Lisa peered back toward the meeting spot, now just a distant enclave of shadows and secrets. Her eyes danced over every possible vantage point, searching for signs of movement, of being watched. But there was only the serene stillness of nature, unaware and indifferent to the human treachery it harbored.

Convinced of her solitude, Lisa turned away from the site. Her movements were swift and silent as she hurried toward her car in the parking lot out front of the mill. The adrenaline pumping through her veins sang a song of both triumph and trepidation. She knew the battle had only just begun, but armed with the truth, Lisa Thompson was a force that even Sheriff Jim would soon reckon with.

The first light of dawn found Lisa in her kitchen, the gentle hum of the refrigerator offering a soothing counterpoint to the thunderous beat of her heart. As she sipped her coffee, the steam curled upwards, mingling with the resolve etched into the furrows of her brow. She knew what needed to be done—confronting Sheriff Jim was a gambit fraught with peril, but it was one she could not shy away from.

She settled into a chair, the creak of the aged wood beneath her a familiar comfort. Her mind raced through scenarios, each potential conversation with the sheriff playing out like a chess match where every move could lead to checkmate. She needed incontrovertible proof of his guilt, something that would stand up beyond the shadow of doubt... or his admittance of guilt.

"Protect and serve," she whispered to herself, echoing the very oath Jim Coleman had taken. The irony was not lost on her; she would protect her family and serve justice, even if it meant facing down the man who had sworn to do the same for their town.

Lisa's fingers danced over her phone, typing out the

message with deliberation. "Sheriff, there's something about Michelle's case we didn't see before. Can you meet me at the old mill ASAP? There's privacy, and I can show you what I've found."

After hitting send, she placed the phone on the table, feeling its weight as though it were an anchor in the storm of her thoughts. She rehearsed her expressions in the reflection of the dark window pane, schooling her features into a mask of innocence and ignorance. She was sure—or at least she hoped and prayed—that he believed she hadn't seen his face when he attacked her at Maggie's house.

The phone vibrated, its movement small but significant. She read the reply: "Lisa, I'll be there. We need to get to the bottom of this."

A mirthless smile touched her lips. If only he knew how deep the bottom was.

For one suspended moment, she allowed herself to feel the warmth of the sun streaming through the window, the golden rays casting patterns across the tabletop. It was a simple pleasure, a reminder of life's quiet beauty amidst the chaos she was about to invite.

She dressed in layers, practicality dictating her choices, and pocketed a small recording device. It was her backup plan—insurance in the form of technology in case he took her phone.

Before stepping out, she paused at the threshold of each of her children's rooms, watching them sleep in peaceful oblivion. In those silent sanctuaries, she renewed her vow to fight for their future, no matter the cost. Oliver was lost in sleep in their mutual bed, which she had come back to after the attack. He would only try and stop her. He no longer thought it was worth the fight, not after she was attacked. So she decided not to tell him.

With a deep breath, Lisa closed the door behind her, the click of the latch sounding like the starting gun of a race, at least in her ears. The thrill of the chase pulsed through her veins as she drove toward the old mill, a place where history stood still amid the whispers of the past.

The rendezvous point loomed ahead, its weathered timbers and silent machinery the witnesses to what would unfold. Lisa parked her car, the crunch of gravel under the tires breaking the hush of morning. She stepped out, her eyes scanning the tree line for any sign of Sheriff Jim's arrival.

The old mill loomed over them like a silent sentinel, its walls etched with secrets of the past. Lisa stood in the shadow of its vast entrance, her breath condensing in the crisp morning air. Sheriff Jim's imposing figure approached, his footsteps deliberate and cautious on the frost-kissed ground.

"Morning, Lisa," he greeted, tipping his hat with a practiced courtesy that didn't quite reach his eyes. "Heard you had something urgent to discuss?"

Lisa's heart hammered against her ribs, but her

voice was steady as she replied, "Yes, Jim. It's about Michelle."

The sheriff's posture stiffened, his hands instinctively clasping behind his back—a defensive gesture that did not escape Lisa's perceptive gaze. She reached into her coat, producing an envelope swollen with potential ruin for the man before her.

"Michelle deserved better," Lisa said, her words edged with cold determination. She handed him the envelope. "And I intend to ensure she gets justice."

Sheriff Jim's fingers hesitated before taking the offering, his expression unreadable. As he tore it open, his eyes scanned the contents: the Polaroid photographs, the written testimonies from the town where she had lived, where they said they had seen him and her together, the witness's account written out as Ramirez had told it to her—all painting a damning picture of the night Michelle died.

"What is this?" he asked.

She also showed him the print of the newspaper article she carried with her. "It was this that led me to Enistown, where Michelle was living, or rather hiding with her son."

He sighed. "What are you talking about? Could you make it quick? I have places to be."

"The article is a story about a young woman from Enistown who was arrested for speeding between Mapletown and Enistown by a certain Sheriff Coleman. And then she was raped. In the middle of the road, she was pulled out of her car and raped in the grass on the cold ground. She reported it, but nothing came of it. The story was hushed because of who the perpetrator was—you. She went to the newspapers with the story, but still, no one dared to touch you. That's how big you are around here. Right? So, you did it again. A few years later, Michelle was driving the same stretch of road, and she was stopped. She was 17 at the time. She was also drunk and known as a party girl around town. So, you raped her, then took her home to her parents, telling them that next time you'd have to take her in. You thought she wouldn't remember, or at least no one would believe her if she did. But she wrote it all down in her diary, Jim. She remembered every little nasty detail, down to your smell and the look in your eyes, as is common for rape victims."

"This is nonsense," he snarled, the photos quivering in his grasp. "You really think I had anything to do with this?"

"Yes," Lisa said. "You got her pregnant, and that's why she had to leave town. Because she confronted you with this news, and you told her you'd kill her and the baby if she didn't terminate the pregnancy. It's all in her journal. "

"Well, she was lying. She was just a young girl. How can you believe something she scribbled in her little book at the age of 17?"

"Well, I know for a fact that she had the child. He lives with the man in Enistown with whom she fell in love when escaping your grip. For ten years, she kept to herself with her happy family until one day, you found her at the bar and asked about the child. Did she tell you there was no child? That she had terminated the pregnancy? To make sure you would stop looking for Sammy, huh? Because, if so, that's when she lied. There's a little boy out there with your DNA in him, enough to prove that you did actually rape her on that day she described. But she was scared you'd come after her and find him. So, when you found her hiding place, you left her with only one option. She had to leave her family. She went to hide in the mountains, in the old abandoned cabin that hardly anyone knew about. But you followed her there, and then you murdered her to keep her from telling the truth. Now, I bet you thought that would be the end of it—that your secret was safe. But it's not. I know everything, and I'm not the only one."

"Be careful, Lisa." The sheriff's voice dropped an octave, a dark undertone threading through his words. "Accusations like these—they're dangerous."

Lisa met his glare, unflinching in her resolve. "Not as dangerous as the truth you've been hiding. I won't let fear dictate what's right."

The air between them crackled with tension, each knowing the stakes had risen beyond their control. Yet, amid the threat and the chill of the wind, Lisa's spirit burned fiercely, a beacon of hope in the pursuit of justice for Oliver's sister.

"Is this how you keep your town safe, Jim? By silencing those who trusted you?" Lisa pressed, keeping one hand tucked out of sight inside her coat pocket. The hidden recording app on her phone was capturing every syllable with crisp clarity—a digital net silently ensnaring the truth. She had also turned on the recording device that Travis gave her, just in case something happened to the phone.

Sheriff Jim's jaw clenched, his weathered face a mask of barely restrained fury. "You know, it's not just about what's legal—it's about what's best for everyone," he said, the words slipping through his teeth like venom. "Sometimes... sacrifices must be made."

Lisa's heart thrummed in her chest, gripping onto his confession like a lifeline amidst the roiling sea of danger surrounding her. She knew she couldn't let her fear show; her children needed their mother to come home tonight.

"Michelle was no sacrifice," she replied evenly, her eyes locking onto his. "She was a person, and whatever your twisted sense of duty told you, you had no right. You killed her."

The sheriff leaned forward, his shadow looming over Lisa as if trying to swallow her whole. "I did what I had to do. And if you think you're walking out of here with that information—"

His threat hung in the air, unfinished but understood. Lisa felt the chill of it against her skin, a stark reminder of the lengths a desperate man might go to protect himself, the length to which he had already gone.

Heart pounding, she measured each breath, each blink, knowing that her next moves would be critical. Her mind raced, plotting an escape that left no trace of her presence in this secluded spot where only the pines were witness to their deadly dance.

"Whatever happens now, the truth will come out," Lisa stated with quiet conviction, her voice steady despite the adrenaline coursing through her veins.

"Be smart, Jim. Don't add my blood to your hands," she added, the implied warning clear in her tone.

With a nod so slight it was almost imperceptible, she signaled her farewell to Sheriff Jim. Turning on her heel, she walked briskly toward the door, her senses heightened to every creak of the old wooden building, every rustle of the wind outside.

"No one will believe you. You can't prove a darn thing!" he yelled after her. "I have many friends in this town. You're a dead woman, Lisa."

Once outside, Lisa slipped into the shadows that clung to the side of the building, her movements deliberate and silent. She retraced her steps, cautious to avoid leaving any sign of her passing. Each footfall was placed with care, avoiding twigs and leaves that might betray her path.

She reached her car, parked a safe distance away, concealed by the thick brush. Breathing a sigh of relief, Lisa slid behind the wheel and started the engine, the soft purr a comforting sound in the oppressive silence.

As she drove away from the meeting place, each mile that passed beneath her tires, Lisa dared to hope that she had taken a crucial step toward unraveling the web of lies and bringing justice to light. But the road ahead was long, and she knew the true test of her resolve had only just begun.

Lisa sped down the winding road, her heart pounding. She could barely contain the trembling that threatened to overtake her as she maneuvered the car through the dense forest. The rearview mirror showed no signs of pursuit, but she knew better than to let her guard down.

She drove with purpose, her hands gripping the steering wheel with a strength born from fear and determination. The evidence on her phone was incendiary, a ticking bomb that could ignite at any moment, and it needed to be safeguarded. Lisa's mind raced with scenarios, each more harrowing than the last, but her resolve was unyielding.

Finally reaching a nondescript cabin, she parked the car and cut the engine. This was Travis's place—a sanctuary away from prying eyes. Travis had been there for her before, a steady presence in the turbulent sea of her past. She trusted him implicitly. She couldn't tell him about her plans of meeting the sherriff, since he wouldn't have let her go. But now, she could.

"Travis," Lisa whispered into her phone, her voice low and urgent, "I have something you need to hear."

"Lisa?" came the immediate response, concern lacing his tone. "Are you all right?"

"Can't talk long. Meet me at your cabin. It's about Jim."

"Understood. Be careful, Lisa."

The call ended, and for a brief moment, Lisa allowed herself to lean back against the headrest, closing her eyes. The danger was palpable, the risk all too real, but the warmth in Travis's voice reminded her that she wasn't alone.

When Travis arrived, his expression was grave. They walked into his old fishing cabin by the lake and sat down. Lisa handed him the phone without a word, watching as he listened to the recording, his brow furrowing deeper with every passing second. When it finished, he looked up at her, the weight of their situation reflected in his eyes.

"We need to protect this evidence," he said, his voice low. "Make copies and store them somewhere safe."

"Already did," Lisa replied, her voice steely with conviction, showing him the recording device that he had given to her. She had come too far to falter now. "And I uploaded everything to the cloud on my phone, so it's still there if anything happens to my phone or me."

As Travis set to work securing the digital files in multiple locations on his laptop as well, Lisa sat by the cold fireplace, her thoughts drifting to her family. Ethan, Abigail, Julia, and Daniel—her reason for being, her reason for fighting. She couldn't let the shadows of this small town snuff out their light.

She thought of Oliver's sister, of the life brutally cut short, and of the son left motherless by a man sworn to protect. Her jaw clenched at the thought of Sheriff Jim's betrayal, the corruption festering beneath his badge. No, she wouldn't stand idly by while injustice reigned.

"Lisa," Travis said, pulling her from her reverie. "It's done. What's our next move?"

"Expose him," Lisa answered without hesitation, her eyes hardening with resolve. "We take everything we have to the authorities outside this town."

"Risky," Travis cautioned, "but I'm with you."

"Good," Lisa said, a small, determined smile tugging at her lips. "Because I'm not stopping until justice is served—for her, this town, and my family."

Travis nodded, understanding the unspoken words that hung in the air between them. This was more than a quest for justice; this was a mother, a survivor, standing against the darkness, refusing to yield.

And so, with the evidence secured and a plan taking shape, Lisa readied herself for what lay ahead. There would be trials and dangers untold, but the flame of truth burned brightly within her.

Chapter Thirteen

The heels of Lisa Thompson's boots clicked against the damp asphalt with an urgent rhythm, breaking the silence of the dimly lit street as she got out of the car and rushed toward her home. Her breath formed misty clouds that trailed behind her, much like the unsettling sensation that someone was tailing her every step. She wrapped her coat tighter around her slender frame, a feeble barrier against the chilling autumn air and the rising dread gnawing at her insides.

Lisa's heart pounded, a frantic drumbeat syncing with her brisk footsteps. Memories of her violent past flashed in her hazel eyes, igniting a familiar flame of determination. She had fought too hard for her family's sanctuary to let darkness encroach upon it now. With Ethan, Abigail, Julia, and Daniel at home, worlds away from this creeping menace, her maternal instincts were a force fiercer than any fear.

Glancing over her shoulder, she searched the

shadows for the source of her unease. The quaint store-fronts of the town offered no clues, their windows dark and serene. The street was an empty canvas, undis-turbed but for the occasional swirl of newly fallen snow twirling across her path. Yet, the absence of evidence did nothing to calm the prickling on the back of her neck; if anything, it amplified the silent alarm blaring inside her.

Quickening her pace, Lisa's mind raced as fast as her steps. She could almost hear Oliver's soothing voice telling her it was just her imagination, but the convic-tion in her gut told her otherwise. In a place where everyone knew each other's secrets, Lisa's recent meddling in matters long buried made her far too conspicuous. And now, it seemed, those secrets were shadowing her through the town. Sheriff Coleman had many friends here; he was right about that. It felt as if eyes from every building were leering down at her.

Her thoughts flickered to the cozy café she co-owned with Oliver. It was their haven, a symbol of the resilience and warmth that shielded their family. But even the thought of the café's welcoming glow couldn't dispel the icy tendrils of fear that slithered up her spine.

Lisa veered off the main road, her boots slick on the icy cobblestone as she slipped into the shadowed embrace of an alley, the newly fallen snow crunching under her feet. The alley was a labyrinthine network of passages sprawled behind the town's quaint facades, and she knew them well; they were the arteries that connected the lifeblood of the community. Now, they offered a slim chance at anonymity and escape.

She ducked behind weathered crates stacked haphazardly by the back door of Mr. Henley's antique shop, her chest tight with alarm. The scent of mildew and old wood filled her nostrils as she crouched low, her fingers grazing the rough surface of the crate's edges. Lisa's breaths came in jagged bursts, each exhale forming fleeting clouds in the chill air.

Although strained to their limit, her ears picked up the subtle encroachment of footsteps, deliberate and steady. They reverberated off the close walls, a sinister drumbeat heralding an unseen threat. The sound seemed to draw nearer with every thump of her racing heart.

She thought of Ethan's laughter, Abigail's curious eyes, Julia's tender grip, and Daniel's earnest attempts to fit into their patchwork family. For them, she'd walk through fire—or hide in alleys. Their faces etched into her resolve, she fumbled for her phone, its screen a beacon of hope.

Her thumb hovered over the emergency call button with practiced swiftness, ready to summon aid with a single press. The footsteps grew louder, echoing like a warning chime. Lisa's grip on the device was a lifeline, the weight of it both a comfort and a burden. She would defend her children and her sanctuary with every fiber of her being. Oliver had given her strength, but it was love that honed it to a point sharper than any fear.

The alley held its breath, the silence between footfalls stretching thin and taut. Lisa waited, every muscle coiled, a mother lioness concealed in the urban underbrush. The shadows around her felt alive, pulsating with the tension of the chase. This small town, with its picturesque charm and hidden rot, was a chessboard, and Lisa was done being a pawn.

The footsteps stopped, and for a heartbeat, the world stilled—then the pursuit resumed, the sound growing ever closer, a crescendo of impending confrontation.

The stillness shattered as a figure materialized. The sheriff stood there, the familiar sternness of his visage twisted into a sinister smile that didn't reach his cold eyes. Lisa's heart, already racing, skipped a beat at the sight of him—Sheriff Coleman, a pillar of their small community, now the harbinger of her deepest fears.

"Lisa," he drawled, the warmth he once offered during town hall meetings gone, replaced with a chilling timbre that seemed to crawl along the alley's brick walls. "You can't escape me."

A shiver raced down Lisa's spine as she clutched the phone like a shield. She could see it now—the malice in his gaze, the gleam of knowing.

His voice cut through the silence again, each word a venomous drop into the cold air.

"You should have stayed out of things that don't

concern you." The threat hung between them, stark and unyielding.

Her mind screamed for action, for escape, but her body resisted, momentarily paralyzed by the gravity of the situation. This was no longer a simple game of cat and mouse; this was survival. Oliver's blue eyes, the warmth of her children's embraces, the love that filled their home—that was what she needed to protect and the reason she had to find a way out of this tightening snare.

Sheriff Coleman's approach was methodical, a predator confident in his impending victory. However, Lisa Thompson was not prey to be cornered and devoured without a fight. Her resolve hardened; the love for her family was a flame that fear could not extinguish.

With every heartbeat pounding in her ears, Lisa prepared to make a stand. Not here, not now, she vowed. Lisa Thompson's story would not end in an alley with whispered threats. It would be a tale of courage, of a mother's love triumphing over the lurking shadows of malice.

Lisa's muscles tensed as she sensed the sheriff's presence closing in. She could almost feel the heat of his breath, the looming threat of his authority and power. Her instincts screamed at her to move, to flee, to survive.

Suddenly, Sheriff Coleman's hand shot out, large and grasping, aiming to snatch her arm and shackle her freedom. But Lisa, powered by a primal surge of fear and determination, jerked her arm away. The tips of his fingers brushed against the fabric of her sleeve—a ghostly caress that promised danger.

She heard his grunt of frustration, a guttural sound muffled by the snow, as she twisted free from his looming figure and began to run. Lisa's feet found their rhythm on the uneven ground, propelling her out of the alley with the force of a river breaking through a dam.

Lisa was not deterred. She ran with the ferocity of a storm, relentless and untamed. Every stride was a drumbeat in the quiet town, every gasp for air a whisper of resistance.

Her thoughts were scattered like leaves in the wind, yet one image remained clear—her children's faces, eyes wide with trust and love. They were her beacon, her reason to push beyond the limits of fear and exhaustion. Oliver's warm smile and steady hands seemed to reach out to her, urging her onward, and it steeled her resolve.

The pursuit was a blur of motion and emotion, a dance with danger where each step could be her last. Yet, within this whirlwind, there was an exhilarating clarity. Lisa felt every heartbeat, every pulse of adrenaline that coursed through her veins, fueling her flight from the man who had sworn to protect but now sought to ensnare.

Each corner she turned was a gamble, each shadow

a potential ally or foe. But the love for her family and Oliver gave her speed, and the memories of her past struggles lent her cunning. Lisa Thompson would not be easily cowed; she was a survivor, a mother, and now, a fugitive racing toward the unknown.

Lisa's feet pounded against the cold pavement, each step a drumbeat of escape as she merged with the flow of townsfolk in the morning bustle. The market square was alive with energy that felt both suffocating and liberating. People milled about, lost in the trivialities of their own lives—laughing, bargaining, utterly oblivious to the peril snapping at Lisa's heels.

She wove through clusters of chattering locals, her gaze fixed on the worn cobblestones, willing herself to become just another face in the crowd. She kept her head down, the shoulder-length strands of her brown hair curtaining her hazel eyes from view. The warmth of human presence around her was a stark contrast to the icy fear that clutched at her heart.

Her chest heaved with exertion, and her lungs burned from the frigid air and relentless pace. Lisa dared not let the comforting hum of life around her slow her desperation. Her limbs moved mechanically, muscle memory guiding her through the sea of people as she avoided eye contact, afraid that any connection might shatter her fragile disguise.

Then, with courage born of necessity, Lisa risked a

glance over her shoulder. Her breath hitched, caught between terror and hope. The sea of faces ebbed and flowed, but Sheriff Coleman's stern visage was nowhere to be seen—there was no sign of the graying hair or piercing gaze that had announced danger like a herald of doom.

A sigh escaped her lips—a quiet sound drowned by the cacophony of the market. It was a sigh that bore the weight of her fears and the lightness of momentary reprieve. Her brisk walk tapered to a steadier pace as she allowed herself this small mercy to regain composure. Yet her heart continued its vigilant rhythm, each beat a reminder of the close call.

Though the immediate threat seemed to have vanished into the throng, Lisa knew the respite could be fleeting.

But for a whisper of time, surrounded by the unsuspecting town, Lisa found solace in her anonymity. She blended into the fabric of the community, drawing strength from the very people she aimed to protect. And in that bustling square, amidst the chaos of commerce and camaraderie, Lisa Thompson gathered herself—ready for the next move in her dangerous game.

As she navigated through the crowd, her mind, a fortress of maternal instinct, strategized. Evidence against Sheriff Coleman was out there, scattered like puzzle pieces waiting to be connected. She would need to be cunning, to weave a web of safety around her family while luring the truth into the light.

"Alone, I'm vulnerable," she whispered, feeling the weight of her small-town world on her shoulders. "But together, we're a force that can push back the shadows."

The buzz of the market had dimmed, and Lisa found a secluded bench near an old, gnarled oak tree. It was here, under the guise of rest, that she retrieved her phone with hands that betrayed no tremor. Her thumb hovered over the screen, then decisively pressed the contact named "Maggie." The name alone brought comfort and thoughts of Maggie's steadfast nature, her unwavering support, and the times they'd stood shoulder-to-shoulder against lesser storms.

"Hey, it's me," Lisa murmured when the call connected, her voice a mix of urgency and composure. "I need your help, Maggie. Can you meet me at the café?"

"Of course, Lisa," came the immediate response, tinged with concern but resolute. "I'll be there."

"Thank you," breathed Lisa, ending the call. As she rose from the bench, the vestiges of fear that had clung to her like morning mist began to dissipate. A simmering determination took hold in its place, warming her core with the promise of justice—for her family and herself.

❧

Lisa's footsteps crunched in the snow as she moved briskly through the town's quiet streets. The air, crisp and tinged with the scent of a distant snowfall, brushed against her cheeks, invigorating her resolve. With each step, the comforting weight of her phone in her coat pocket served as a reminder that she was not alone in this fight.

Her eyes, scanned the environment for any hint of movement. Every shadow, every rustling leaf, held the potential for threat, but Lisa's fear had transformed into focus. The same hazel eyes that had warmed hearts within the walls of her café now reflected a steely determination that would have surprised many who thought they knew her.

The familiar outline of the café came into view. Her sanctuary, the café, suddenly became the rallying point for her resistance. Lisa approached the door, her fingers deftly retrieving the key from beneath her shirt, where it lay concealed on a chain around her neck.

She unlocked the door with a soft click, slipped inside, and secured it behind her. The familiar scent of ground coffee and baked goods lingered, a comforting embrace amid the tumult of her reality. She navigated through the chairs upturned on tables, moving on silent feet toward the glow at the back. Upstairs, she could hear the sound of her family's footsteps as the laziness of a Sunday had begun.

"Lisa?" A voice cut through the stillness, low and steady.

"Here, Maggie," Lisa replied, letting a brief smile

touch her lips as she stepped into the muted light of the back room.

Maggie stood by the old wooden table. Lisa told her everything—about the pregnancy, about the meeting with Sheriff Coleman and the recording where he admitted to killing Michelle, and how he had come after her again, trying to stop her.

"I'm in danger, Maggie. And I need your help."

"Of course," she said.

Lisa squeezed back, the warmth from Maggie's hand spreading through her, rekindling the embers of courage within. They were two women bound by more than friendship—a sisterhood forged in adversity.

"Let's get to work," Lisa affirmed, her gaze sweeping over the evidence before them.

This was more than a quest for justice; it was a battle for her family's future, even the town's future. And Lisa Thompson, mother, wife, and reluctant warrior, would not back down. She was ready to face the storm, armed with love as her shield and truth as her sword.

Chapter Fourteen

The silence of the room after Maggie left closed in on Lisa like a tightening vise, suffocating her with its weight. Her mind spun, a maelstrom of terrifying possibilities seizing her thoughts. She saw them vividly—the dangers lurking around every corner of their small town, the shadowy figure of Sheriff Coleman morphing from protector to predator in the blink of an eye. Ethan, Abigail, Daniel, Julia... each child's face flickered before her eyes, painted with fear and confusion. The thought of her family being harmed because of her knowledge was unbearable.

"Please, no," she whispered to the empty room, her voice barely breaking the hush that hung in the air. Her fingers instinctively curled around the fabric of her shirt, right over her heart, as if she could physically hold together the pieces that threatened to shatter. The tightness in her chest was relentless, a cruel reminder of her vulnerability in the face of a man who wielded his power with ruthless precision.

Lisa's breaths came quicker now, shallow and jagged. But as each one fought its way into her lungs, it also brought with it a spark—a spark of defiance that refused to be snuffed out. She couldn't afford to crumble; her children needed her courage and her resolve.

Her hands, though trembling, were driven by an urgency that cut through the fog of fear. She reached for her laptop, the cool metal casing familiar under her fingertips. Powering it up, Lisa's gaze fixed on the screen, watching as the digital world blinked to life before her. This machine, so often a tool for mundane tasks, was now her lifeline—the vessel for her testament.

With each click of the keys, Lisa poured out her story along with the evidence she had meticulously gathered against Sheriff Coleman. Every encounter, veiled threat, and piece of proof pointing to his dark deeds flowed onto the screen in a torrent of desperate honesty. She recounted the night he had cornered her, the glint of malicious intent in his eyes as clear as the badge on his chest. The memory made her sick to her stomach, but she pushed through, documenting each detail before they could be lost to time—or worse, to the silencing grip of corruption.

She knew the risks, the danger of what she was doing. If Coleman discovered her actions, it would not just be her own life in jeopardy. But the alternative—staying silent, allowing his reign of terror to continue unchecked—was unthinkable. She was Lisa Thompson, a mother, a wife, and a woman who had stared down the abyss before and emerged stronger for it. Her love for her family was a shield, her will to protect them as unyielding as the mountains that cradled their town.

"Let this be enough," she prayed silently, not to any god in particular, but to the universe, to the forces of good that she hoped still lingered in the world. "Let this be the beginning of the end for him."

As she hit "send" on the document, sending it all to the local newspaper, Lisa felt a tremor of anticipation mingled with her dread. The next steps were unclear, the path fraught with peril, but she had made the first move in the deadly chess game against a foe masquerading as a guardian of the law. And she would not back down.

The coolness of the hallway floor seeped through Lisa's bare feet as she tiptoed away from the chaos of her own thoughts later that evening, seeking refuge in the silence of slumbering innocence. The door to Abigail's room creaked open, a familiar soundtrack to the secret night watches Lisa had kept since her daughter was born. Abigail lay there, cocooned in dreams beneath a quilt of pastel hues, her chest rising and falling with the gentle rhythm of untroubled sleep.

Lisa approached the bedside, her silhouette a quiet guardian cast by the moonlight that slipped through the window. She reached out, her fingers brushing a rogue strand of brown hair from Abigail's forehead, the action grounding her in the now. The simple touch was a talisman against the fear that clawed at her insides—a silent vow to shield her child from the shadows that lurked beyond the safety of these four walls.

A sigh escaped Lisa's lips as she gazed down at Abigail, whose features, so reminiscent of her own, were softened in repose. The sight of her daughter, so serene, stirred a well of protectiveness within Lisa that was fierce enough to banish demons, strong enough to challenge even the untouchable sheriff who threatened their peace.

Turning away from the bed, Lisa's gaze landed on a family photo perched on the bedside table. It was a snapshot of a sun-drenched day, all smiles and laughter, with Ethan's arm slung carelessly around Daniel's shoulder and Julia's hand clasped in Oliver's. It was a portrait of joy, an emblem of love's resilience.

Her fingers traced the edge of the frame, warmth blooming in her chest as she remembered the summer day it was taken—the picnic at the lake, the sound of her children's giggles mingling with the lapping of water on the shore. That day, they had been invincible, untouched by the sinister undercurrents of small-town secrets.

Clutching the frame a little tighter, Lisa allowed the memory to fill her with renewed vigor.

She set the picture back down gently, a whisper of a smile playing on her lips. There was no backing down, not when so much was at stake. With the image of her family's boundless happiness etched into her mind, Lisa felt the flicker of hope fan into a flame, casting light on the determination etched deep in her soul.

"Whatever it takes," she breathed to the silent room, her heart echoing the promise. "I will keep you safe."

She then walked into the living room, where Oliver had fallen asleep on the couch in front of the TV. Her first instinct was to look for a bottle of alcohol, but to her joy, she found none. He had been keeping his promise to her for weeks now, which made her love him even more. She woke him up with a soft kiss on his lips, and he blinked happily, coming back to reality.

"Lisa?" Then, he smiled.

"It's time we talk," she said. "I have a lot to tell you."

Chapter Fifteen

Oliver's footsteps were a rhythmic thrum against the worn wooden planks of their living room floor. With each pass from the tattered couch to the stone-cold fireplace, his boots whispered across the grain, a stark contrast to the chaos thundering in his head. He couldn't believe the story Lisa had just told him. He was angry with her for going behind his back and putting herself in danger; for that, he was furious, but deep down, he couldn't help but be a little proud of her for getting the recordings. She told him she had sent it all to the local newspaper, and hopefully, they'd run the story. Oliver was afraid of what kind of storm they were facing.

"Why would you do that?" he asked.

"We can't very well go to the police, can we?" she added.

"You've put us all in danger, Lisa," he said. "I don't

like it. The sheriff has a lot of friends around here. They'll go to great lengths to protect him. You don't know if the editors at the paper are on his side."

His mind raced with worry, the same way it did when the sea turned merciless.

"Oliver," Lisa said, her breath coming in short, sharp intakes. "I couldn't just... he murdered your sister. And then he covered it all up. He raped her and tried to make her get rid of the child. He's done it to another woman too, maybe even more."

"I can't believe you went to meet him," he said, sounding angrier than he was. He was more worried. What did this mean for them now? For their family? "He could have killed you. Why didn't you tell me?"

"Because you would have stopped me. Michelle's boy...." Lisa's voice broke, the fragments laced with horror. "Sammy. He's your nephew, Oliver. The sheriff... he killed Michelle because that boy is proof—proof that he raped her. And now, Sammy is in danger, too."

Oliver's heart thudded painfully against his ribcage, the implications of Lisa's words spreading through him like wildfire.

"We agreed," he said. "We agreed when he attacked you to leave it alone. It was too dangerous. We have children, and yet you... you... you've put us all in great danger. We risk losing everything we've built—the café and the life we have with our children. How could you do that to us?"

A shudder racked her body. "He came after me

again, Oliver. I managed to escape, but he's after me. He wants to silence me. I'm terrified for Ethan, for Abigail, Julia, for Daniel.... I know you asked me to stop, but I couldn't. How could I?" Her voice cracked, dissolving into sobs.

Oliver stared at her, his fists clenching. All he wanted was to forget the whole thing. Once he realized it was the sheriff in those Polaroid pictures, he knew they were up against someone stronger than themselves, someone too powerful, and it wouldn't be worth the fight. Oliver wasn't ready to lose everything for this. He had hit rock bottom and just come back and turned his life around again. He was on the right track. And now this? It was all destroyed again. Oliver sighed and glanced toward the liquor cabinet, craving a drink to calm his nerves. Luckily, it was empty and had been since he threw it all out after deciding enough was enough. Lisa's big eyes stared up at him, awaiting his response, his love. How could he not give it to her?

Oliver wrapped his arms around Lisa, pulling her close and feeling her tremble against him. His mind churned with the need to act, to protect the woman he loved and the life they had built together. Fear clawed at him, but beneath it all, a fierce determination began to smolder. Tomorrow, they would meet with Travis, and they would form a plan—a plan to bring the truth to light and keep their family safe. He would know what to do.

But for tonight, he held Lisa, his embrace a fortress

against the darkness encroaching upon their small-town existence. It was love entwined with fear, heart-warming yet chilling, as they stood together on the precipice of a battle neither of them had asked for but were both ready to fight.

Chapter Sixteen

The crunch of snow beneath their boots was the only sound in the cold twilight air as Oliver and Lisa made their way to the secluded fishing cabin by the lake nestled amongst towering pines. Tension hung between them like a third companion, both of them armed with the heavy knowledge of who had brought terror to their small town. Oliver's hand found Lisa's, his grip firm yet reassuring as if he could squeeze out the fear that threatened to paralyze them both.

"I'm here for you," Oliver whispered, his voice laced with a cocktail of determination and concern that was as familiar to Lisa as the contours of his face. "Always and forever."

Lisa nodded, her eyes mirroring the resolve she saw in him. She felt the weight of the past and her history of violence that had taught her to be guarded, casting a shadow over her heart. But there was something else there, too, kindled by Oliver's unwavering support—a spark of courage that refused to be extinguished.

They neared the cabin. It stood as a silent sentinel, promising either sanctuary or peril. Their steps slowed, caution threading through their bodies as they surveyed the scene. The door—a rough-hewn slab of wood that should have been secured against the night—stood inexplicably ajar.

"Travis would never leave it open like that," Oliver muttered under his breath, his brows knitting together in a frown.

"No, he wouldn't," Lisa agreed, her pulse quickening as she clutched the strap of the bag slung across her shoulder.

Oliver's woodworking-honed muscles tensed, ready for whatever lay ahead. He exhaled slowly, his breath visible in the chill air, and stepped forward. Lisa followed, her own body coiled tight with adrenaline. They shared a glance, both sets of eyes communicating a wordless pact—they were in this together, no matter what awaited them inside.

With each step closer to the threshold, the suspense twisted tighter, the unknowns multiplying like shadows at dusk. But amidst the thrill of the impending confrontation, there was an undercurrent of warmth that only two hearts weathering a storm together could understand.

Oliver reached out and pushed the door wider, its creaking hinges singing a foreboding note into the stillness of the evening. They crossed the threshold, stepping into the unknown.

The floorboards groaned under Oliver's weight as he stepped into the cabin, a stark contrast to the silent dread that hung in the air. He let his eyes roam quickly over the interior, instincts sharpened by years of braving the unpredictable sea now tuned to the more immediate danger lurking within these walls. The musky scent of aged wood mingled with something metallic, a tang that set his nerves on edge.

Lisa's presence was a palpable force at his back; her breathing was shallow and quick, but her resolve was just as firm as his own. They moved together, seamless as a tide drawn by the moon's unseen pull—two halves of a whole facing the tempest.

There, in the dim light filtering through the dust-streaked windows, sat Travis. He was bound to a chair, his rugged face etched with lines of tension, his eyes a silent alarm. The sight struck a chord of trepidation in Oliver's chest, a note that resonated with every beat of his heart.

"Travis," Lisa whispered, her voice a mix of relief and fear, a beacon reaching out for connection in the gloom.

Before another word could part from her lips, the door behind them swung shut with a resounding crash that fractured the silence like a gunshot. Oliver whirled around, his protective instinct flaring bright and hot, only to find the source of their nightmare standing between them and their only exit.

Sheriff Coleman loomed like an ominous cliff against the stormy sea. His shadow stretched across the floor, darkening the room with the weight of betrayal. It was a scene that mocked every sense of security they had ever known.

"Jim?" Lisa's voice cracked, laden with disbelief and burgeoning panic.

Oliver's mind raced, every warning signal blaring as he took in the sight of the handcuffs securing Travis to the chair—their ally rendered helpless by the very hands meant to uphold justice.

"It's a setup," Oliver growled, his gaze darting around the room, searching for any advantage, weapon, or means of escape. His fingers itched for the familiar feel of his woodworking tools, for anything that could be wielded to defend his family, to carve out their survival in this dire twist of fate.

"Oliver...." Lisa's hand found his, gripping it with a strength born of desperation and love, her touch grounding him amid the chaos.

The flicker of the light switch was brief yet ominous—a stutter of light that preluded darkness. It descended upon the room with voracious speed, swallowing shadows and shapes until Oliver and Lisa stood blind in the belly of the cabin. They clung to each other, two silhouettes adrift in an ocean of black, their breaths shallow drafts in the silence.

"Stay close," Oliver whispered, his voice a low rumble in her ear. His fingers tightened around hers, their calluses a testament to years of crafting safety from wood and love. He remembered the cabin's layout, every corner and crevice from when he'd helped Travis with repairs. With each step, he felt for the familiar, willing his eyes to pierce the dark.

Lisa's heart thrummed against her ribcage, the beat a relentless drum that countered the stillness. Her mind flashed through memories—narrow escapes, close calls, moments when life hung on a knife's edge. She had faced her demons before and survived them with grit and grace, but this was different. This was home, tainted by terror.

"Oliver, I—" Her words fractured as a new presence emerged, a cold whisper that slithered across her senses.

"Ah, the lovely couple." The voice was a shard of ice cutting through the thick air. "So determined, so brave—it's almost a shame."

Sheriff Jim Coleman stepped from the embrace of shadows, his form outlined by the faintest glimmer of light from a lamp outside. The blade gleamed in his hand—a cruel silver curve that promised pain. Lisa's pulse quickened; she knew the menace that waited in that steel.

"Jim, why?" Oliver's query was half-plea and half-accusation, a demand for answers where none could satisfy. "I have known you my entire life."

"Because you can't have light without the dark," came the reply, cryptic and cold. "And because I can."

Oliver positioned himself between Lisa and the looming figure, his stance solid despite the trembling ground of betrayal beneath him. His life, spent navigating tumultuous seas and shaping stubborn wood, had honed his resolve. He would not let this darkness consume them.

"Lisa, behind me," he instructed, though it was more a comfort than command. He felt her nod against his back, her presence a fierce flame in the encroaching night.

"Bravery won't save you," taunted Coleman, the knife dancing in his grip, a serpent poised to strike.

"Maybe not," Oliver conceded, his voice steady. "But love will."

In those words lay their defiance, a declaration that they would not be undone by fear or malice. Together, Oliver and Lisa stood ready to face the abyss, their bond a beacon that no darkness could extinguish. Their love was a fortress, and within its walls, they prepared to defend the future they had built with every scrap of courage they possessed.

Then, Coleman swung the knife.

Oliver's breaths came in ragged gasps as he dodged another vicious swipe of the knife, his movements a testament to years of physical labor on the docks and in the workshop. The blade cut through the air, a whisper away from flesh. Lisa's eyes darted around, her mind racing for a solution, her body taut with adrenaline.

"Oliver!" she cried out as the sheriff feinted left and lunged right, the knife's edge glinting dangerously close to Oliver's arm. He staggered back just in time, his hands seeking any advantage, his fingers brushing against the rough wood of the cabin's interior.

The dance of death continued, Coleman's laughter slicing through the tension as sharply as the weapon he wielded. Lisa watched, heart pounding, as Oliver narrowly avoided another strike, his footing almost betraying him.

It was now or never.

Her gaze fell on the remnants of a chair, shattered in the commotion—a leg lying innocently beside the overturned table. She lunged for it without hesitation, her fingers wrapping around the splintered wood. The weight of it felt reassuring, grounding amidst the chaos.

"Hey!" she shouted, her voice laced with fear and determination. As Coleman turned toward her, distracted by the challenge, she swung with all the might her café days and protective maternal instincts had instilled in her.

The chair leg connected with the assailant's wrist, a satisfying crack echoing through the room as the knife clattered to the floor. The world seemed to pause for a split second, the balance of power teetering on a precipice.

Seizing the moment, Oliver barreled into the killer

with the force of an Atlantic gale, his body driven by the primal need to protect his family—his love for Lisa transforming into raw kinetic energy. They hit the ground hard, the killer's breath huffing out in surprise.

Lisa watched as Oliver pinned the assailant beneath him, every muscle in his body straining to maintain control.

"Call for help," he grunted, his focus unyielding as he wrestled to keep the killer subdued.

But Lisa couldn't tear her gaze away from Oliver, who stood as a bastion of safety in their turbulent lives, now grappling with the embodiment of their night-mares. Together, they were a symphony of survival, their love the melody that played on despite the dark-ness that sought to silence it.

Panic still clawed at her throat, but the sight of Oliver's unwavering resolve steeled her spirit. This was their life, their love, their fight—and together, they were unstoppable.

Oliver's arms tensed, his grip on the killer's wrists like iron bands. But in a desperate contortion, the assailant twisted free, sending Oliver stumbling. Time fractured as Lisa's scream pierced the air, her terror a tangible force.

The killer surged forward, knife glinting anew in the dim light, aiming for Lisa's heart. But Oliver, propelled by an instinct as deep as the ocean he once sailed, launched himself into the blade's path. The edge bit into him, stealing his breath, pain flaring where flesh gave way to unyielding intention.

"Oliver!" Lisa cried out, her voice a beacon in the sudden storm of chaos.

Her world narrowed to the sight of Oliver's crumpled form, to the blood that started to stain his shirt—a crimson testament to his sacrifice. Heat seared through her veins, love and fear melding into a singular force that drove her forward. A mother and a wife—her roles fused into a shield of fierce resolve.

"Get away from him!" she roared, her voice echoing off the cabin walls with an authority born of battles past and present.

She swung the broken chair leg with all the might her trembling muscles could muster, her strike an arrow loosed from the bow of her soul. It connected with a heavy thud against the killer's temple. He staggered, stunned by the ferocity of her retaliation, his eyes clouding with confusion and pain.

Lisa stood over Oliver, her stance unwavering despite the tremble in her limbs. He groaned, attempting to rise, but she gently pushed him back. "Stay down, love. I've got this," she whispered, her gaze never leaving the reeling figure before them.

As the killer swayed, disoriented, Lisa's heart raced with a fusion of fear and triumph. She had defended their life together, their love—a love that was a fortress against the darkness, a warmth in the cold night. Oliver's eyes met hers, pride and gratitude shining even through the veil of his agony.

"Lisa..." he murmured, and she knew then that whatever came next, they would face it as they always had—together, their bond unbreakable.

❧

Blood seeped from Oliver's side, a stark reminder of the sacrifice made just moments ago. But his determination did not wane; if anything, it became steelier. He pushed through the pain, rising to shaky feet with the resolve of a man who had known hardship and heartache but never defeat. Dazed by Lisa's defensive strike, the killer swayed like a tree in a storm, vulnerable to the final blow.

"Oliver, no!" Lisa's voice was a mix of caution and courage, but Oliver knew there was no turning back. With a swift movement, born from years of wrestling the elements at sea, he lunged forward, delivering a decisive punch that connected with the killer's jaw. The thud resonated throughout the cabin, a grim symphony to the end of their terror. The assailant crumpled to the floor, motionless.

"Is he—?" Lisa's question hung in the air, her eyes wide with concern.

"Unconscious," Oliver confirmed, his own breathing ragged.

Together, they moved quickly and efficiently, their motions synchronized by a shared life of overcoming obstacles. They found a rope in the corner of the room and bound the killer's hands securely. Only then did they allow themselves a moment to believe that it was over.

Lisa found her phone, her fingers dancing over the numbers as she dialed for help, her eyes refusing to focus. Her voice was steady as she spoke to the dispatcher, every word laced with the weight of survival.

"Help is on the way," she said to Oliver, reaching out to squeeze his arm, an intimate gesture that spoke volumes of the trust and love woven into their union. They turned to Travis, who sat handcuffed, his veteran's eyes reflecting the night's chaos. Without a word, Oliver retrieved the keys from the unconscious killer's pocket and freed the retired cop. Travis nodded his thanks, his gaze lingering on the couple with a mixture of respect and sorrow for what they had endured.

"Are you two okay?" His voice was gruff but not without warmth.

"We're alive," Oliver replied, his tone containing layers of meaning. "Thanks to each other."

"Look up in the corner," Travis said as Lisa turned the lights on again. They both did and spotted a small camera underneath the ceiling.

Travis smiled secretively. "I'll bet you I got all of that. I think Coleman thought it wouldn't work if he turned the light out, but it isn't just any camera. It's infrared. I guess my years in the force have made me quite paranoid. But how's that for evidence?"

"Amazing," Oliver said. "Simply amazing."

As the adrenaline began to ebb, the full impact of their ordeal settled upon them like a heavy cloak. Oliver and Lisa found solace in each other's embrace, their bodies trembling not just from the exertion but from the flood of emotions that accompanied such a close brush with death. Grief for what had almost been lost mingled with relief that they had triumphed, their love a beacon that had guided them through the darkness.

They stood locked in each other's arms, hearts beating in unison against the backdrop of a battle-scarred room. The fight had taken its toll, yet in that quiet after the storm, there was an unspoken understanding that together, they were invincible. Oliver kissed the top of Lisa's head, a silent vow that echoed through the very walls of the cabin.

The sound of sirens cut through the stillness, piercing the thick tension that hung in the air. Seated on the rough wooden floor of the cabin, back against the wall, Lisa felt Oliver's hand tighten around hers. They exchanged a weary yet resolute glance as they heard the crunch of boots on the snow outside.

"Never thought I'd be so glad to hear sirens," Oliver whispered, his voice a ragged thread of relief woven through the remnants of terror.

Lisa nodded, the corners of her mouth lifting in a

half-smile that didn't quite reach her eyes—eyes that had seen too much but remained luminous with defiant love. Oliver's stab wound was bleeding still, and it worried her.

"Our kids will be happy to see us when we get home," she said softly, her thoughts turning to their children, the innocents who knew nothing of the darkness that had just enveloped their parents' lives while their beloved Aunt Maggie took care of them.

"Everything we did... we did for them," Oliver murmured, pressing his lips to Lisa's forehead, his breath warm against her skin. In the dim light filtering through the windows, his face was etched with pain and pride—pain from the wounds he bore and pride in their shared strength.

"Oliver, our love, it's... it's unbreakable," Lisa breathed out, the realization blooming inside her like the first rays of dawn after an endless night. "We've been through hell, but look at us. We're still standing. Together."

"Always together, forever," Oliver affirmed, his dark eyes shimmering with emotion. "I'll cherish you and Ethan, Abigail, Julia, and Daniel until my last breath. This... all of this has only made me love you more if that's even possible."

Their promise hung in the air, as sacred and enduring as the vows they had once exchanged. It was a bond forged in fire, tempered by adversity, and now unassailable.

Suddenly, the door burst open, flooding the cabin

with light and the voices of the first responders who rushed in. Paramedics moved swiftly to attend to Oliver's injuries while police officers secured the scene. Travis stood up, overseeing the chaos with a veteran's calm, and then he told them everything.

"Mom! Dad!" The plaintive cries of their children cut through the commotion as they returned to the café, and Lisa's heart leaped into her throat. She turned to see Ethan and Abigail, their young faces streaked with tears and worry, rushing toward them with Julia toddling behind, her little arms outstretched.

"Thank God you're safe," Lisa sobbed, pulling her children into a fierce embrace, feeling Oliver's strong arms encircle them all. They clung to each other, a family reunited, their bonds unshakable.

"Your bravery is commendable," Detective Ramirez said, tipping his hat to Oliver and Lisa with a solemn nod. He had taken them home after they had gone to the hospital to get Oliver's wound stitched and then spent hours telling their story—a story that seemed almost unbelievable if it wasn't for the recordings to prove it. "You two are the talk of the town. Everyone's grateful for what you've done."

"Mommy, Daddy, you're heroes!" Daniel exclaimed, his eyes wide with amazement as he hugged his parents tightly.

"Heroes with the strongest love ever," Ethan added, looking up at them with admiration.

"Love that saved us," Abigail chimed in, her voice steady despite the tremble in her hands.

As the last of the squad cars pulled away from their home, Oliver and Lisa stood on the porch, battered bodies leaning against each other for support. The evening sky, painted with strokes of orange and purple as the sun dipped below the horizon, brought a promise of tranquility after the tempest of terror they had weathered.

"Look at that sunset," Lisa murmured, her voice a tender note in the quiet of the twilight. "It's like the world is telling us it's going to be okay."

Oliver wrapped an arm around her shoulders, drawing her closer. His fingers traced the line of her jaw, a silent testament to his awe of her courage. "We made it, Lisa. We faced down our worst nightmare... and we won."

The echo of their children's laughter drifted from inside the house, a soothing balm to the raw edges of their nerves. Each giggle was a reminder of what they had fought for—what they would always fight for. They were survivors, tempered by strife, their love a resilient force that refused to be extinguished.

"Tomorrow," Oliver said, his gaze locking with hers, "we start fresh. No more looking over our shoulders. Just you, me, the kids, and a whole lot of love to go around."

Lisa nodded, her eyes glistening with unshed tears, not of fear, but of hope—a hope as vast as the ocean.

"We've got a lot of healing to do," she conceded, "but with you by my side, I feel like we can conquer anything."

"Anything," Oliver echoed, sealing the vow with a gentle kiss upon her forehead.

Inside the house, their children played, oblivious to the scars their parents bore, both physical and emotional. But those scars would fade, and in their place would grow stories of bravery, of two people who stood against darkness together, their love their greatest weapon.

"Come on," Lisa said, taking his hand in hers, the contact sending warmth spiraling through him, "let's go be with our family."

They stepped across the threshold into the glow of their living room, the heart of their home. It was here, surrounded by the laughter and love of their children, that Oliver and Lisa could finally let the tension ebb from their weary muscles. Here, they could begin to weave the tapestry of their renewed life, each thread a testament to their unbreakable bond.

Tonight, they had defeated death. Tomorrow, they would live—not just survive—in the fullness of the love they had defended so fiercely. Together, they would rebuild, stronger and more united than ever before. And tomorrow, the story would be all over the newspaper and on everyone's lips.

Oliver's hands were gentle as he pulled the quilt up to Julia's chin, her soft breaths already deepening into the rhythm of sleep. Across the room, Lisa hummed a lullaby, a tune as familiar and comforting as the small-town streets they called home. Ethan and Abigail, tucked in their beds, lay still, the day's adventures having finally claimed their boundless energy. In the bed, Daniel's fist clenched and unclenched around his blanket, his eyelids fluttering in the throes of dreamland.

The couple shared a silent exchange, communicating through the subtle language of shared glances and soft smiles that only years of intimacy could perfect. With the children at peace, the night wrapped the house in its quiet embrace.

Lisa caught the shift in Oliver's gaze, the way it darkened with an emotion that sent a tremor of anticipation down her spine. His eyes, so often filled with concern and a haunted past, now danced with a different kind of intensity—one that promised escape and connection in equal measure. He reached out, his calloused hand finding hers, the touch electrifying despite its familiarity.

"Let's make sure the world outside this door stays outside, just for a little while," Oliver whispered, his voice a gravelly melody that stirred the dormant embers of desire within her.

Lisa allowed herself to be led, her feet padding

softly over the hardwood floor as they made their way to the sanctuary of the bathroom. The steam slipped out beneath the door like a secret, curling around their ankles, inviting them into its warm clutches. Oliver pushed the door open, revealing the misty haven where the worries of their small-town lives could be washed away, if only temporarily.

There was something thrilling about the prospect of stealing this moment, a fragile bubble of time untouched by the shadows of their past or the ever-present undercurrents of danger that seemed to lurk just beyond the streetlights' glow. As the shower's rhythmic drumming filled the room, Lisa found herself caught up in the current of Oliver's need, a powerful force that left no room for hesitation or doubt.

"Come on," he said, his voice barely above the sound of cascading water. It wasn't just an invitation but a vow—a silent promise that within the steam and spray, they would find not just each other's bodies but the strength and unity to face any storm that might come their way.

Together, they crossed the threshold, leaving behind the roles of protectors and providers. Tonight, they were simply Oliver and Lisa—imperfect souls bound by a love that thrived amidst the chaos, ready to reaffirm the ties that connected them deeper than the roots of the old oak tree that stood watch over their home.

❧

Steam veiled the room, diffusing the sharp edges of reality as Oliver and Lisa found sanctuary within the shower's embrace. The warm water enveloped them, droplets tracing paths over their skin, whispering away the tensions of the day. In this sequestered space where the steam hung thick and heavy, the world outside ceased to exist.

Oliver's eyes, deep pools of earnest devotion, caught Lisa's gaze. They spoke a silent language only they understood—a dialect of shared hardships and unspoken fears, interlaced with an enduring love that had been their lifeline in a sea of tribulations. He reached for her, his movements deliberate and filled with intent, his calloused fingers a testament to the hard work he poured into every crafted piece and every moment spent for their family.

The water's rhythm became the soundtrack to their closeness, its symphony harmonizing with the beat of two hearts momentarily freed from worry. With a tender urgency, Oliver pressed Lisa against the cool tiles of the shower wall. His hands were gentle yet assured, the skilled hands of a woodworker now exploring the contours of her body with the reverence it deserved.

Lisa's breath hitched as Oliver's lips met hers, each kiss a molten seal of their connection. She could feel the strength in his arms, the same arms that had held her through countless storms—both literal and figurative. The warmth of his touch seared through the veil of vapor, igniting a fervent blaze that promised to keep all the chills of their small-town mysteries at bay.

Their kisses grew deeper, more urgent, each one a crescendo in the quiet symphony of their hidden oasis. As Oliver's hands roamed, reaffirmation was etched into every caress; here was safety, passion, and the steadfast anchor of their mutual resolve. And although the mist obscured their view of the world beyond, within each other's embrace, they saw everything that mattered.

The pulse of the water matched the racing of Lisa's heart, each droplet a sizzling whisper against her skin as Oliver's touch traced paths of fire along her spine. With every press of his fingertips, sparks flew, igniting an inferno within her that had been stoked by years of trust, challenges overcome, and shared secrets in the dead of night. His movements were synchronous with hers, a dance they had perfected through whispers and glances, through protecting their family from the shadows that lurked in their peaceful town.

The steam cloaked them in a world apart, where the thrill of danger that often nipped at their heels dissolved into the heat between them. The cascade of water amplified every sensation, the liquid heat a conduit for their connection, searing away all doubts and fears. It was here, amidst the veil of vapor, that every touch spoke volumes of their unspoken bond, the promise of always finding harbor in one another no matter how tempestuous the seas of life became.

Lisa's fingers clung to Oliver's shoulders, muscles honed from years of carving wood, now sculpting their union with the same fervor and meticulousness. His deft hands, which could tease out the secrets of grain and knot, now explored the landscape of her body with an intimacy that whispered of eternal devotion. The water intensified their every sensation, the sound of it mingling with their quickened breaths, creating a symphony that resonated deep within their souls.

In this hazy cocoon of warmth and moisture, their senses heightened, and they moved together as if guided by an unseen force, a perfect unity forged through the flames of past trials. Each droplet of water seemed to sizzle upon contact, a testament to the heat that radiated from their entwined forms. Here, shielded from the world's prying eyes, they rediscovered the depths of their emotional tether, a bond not even the darkest of secrets could sever.

And though the steam wrapped around them like a shroud, within it, they found a clarity that only true love could unveil—a thrilling sense of completeness that both calmed Lisa's resilient spirit and set it ablaze with a passion as consuming as the mysteries that danced on the edges of their peaceful existence.

The cascade of water enveloped them in its rhythmic torrent, a veil of steam blurring the edges of reality. Amidst this chorus of falling droplets, their whispers carried the weight of unspoken promises and long-held dreams.

"Lisa," Oliver's voice was a tender murmur, blending seamlessly with the pattering symphony around them. "You are my everything, my lighthouse in the dark."

Her response was a breath, a sigh that feathered across his damp skin. "And you, my harbor in the wildest storm," she said, her tone laced with fervor and an undeniable trace of vulnerability. In those words, she laid bare the essence of her trust, hard-won and fiercely guarded.

As the warmth of the water continued to rise like a tide around them, Oliver's hands charted a course along Lisa's body. His fingers traced the contours of her strength, the bold lines of survival that had weathered tempests both within and without. Each touch reverberated through her, a gentle yet insistent affirmation of his claim on her heart.

His palms caressed the slope of her waist, sweeping upwards to the curve of her shoulders—a topography he knew as intimately as the wooden forms he shaped by day. The pressure of his hands was soft but certain, a silent oath that echoed through every inch of her flesh. With every pass, every glide, he seemed to be mapping out a future, one where fear could no longer cast its shadow over their union.

The moment was theirs alone, suspended between passion and peace. Here, sheltered from the whispers of a small town with eyes too keen and memories too long, they found solace in each other's arms. Every shared breath and mingling heartbeat was a testament to what they had built together—something unyielding that defied the odds.

In the sanctuary of their shower, amidst the steam and the sounds of life beyond their walls, Oliver and Lisa shared not just the heat of their bodies but the thrumming excitement of a love that had triumphed over trials. And though the quiet thrill of their intimacy was laced with the suspense of a life lived on the edge of secrets, in this moment, they were untouchable.

Lisa's fingers found sanctuary in the silkiness of Oliver's dark hair, pulling him closer as she surrendered to the rhythm of their connection. The world beyond the shower's embrace dissolved into a hazy afterthought, her senses sharpening to nothing but the man before her and the fervent beat of his heart against hers. Each pulse was a dance, each caress a promise whispered without words.

The steam rose around them, a veil that rendered every touch more profound, every glance more intoxicating. With each droplet of water cascading down their entwined bodies, the heat between them grew as if the very air they breathed stoked the fire of their passion. The mist clung to Lisa's skin, beading like tiny jewels that Oliver's lips sought with tender reverence.

Every movement was a shared secret, a cherished memory in the making, crafting a tapestry of desire that only they could understand. This shower, their secluded haven, became the whole world; there was no past laden with shadows, no threat of future uncertainties. There was only the here and now, the syncopated cadence of their love, a melody played out in touches and sighs.

Oliver's hands traced the length of her spine, drawing shivers that mingled with the warmth of the water. Lisa arched into his touch, letting go of the silent vigilance that so often governed her life. Here, in the protective circle of Oliver's arms, she allowed herself the rare gift of vulnerability, trusting in his strength.

The steamy cocoon enveloped them, a testament to their resilience, a whisper of romance amidst the ever-present thrills and suspense of their existence. It was a dance of contrasts—the cool tiles against their heated skin, the clarity of their bond within the fog. And as they moved together, lost in the rhythm of their love, Lisa felt a thrilling sense of completeness. In this moment, it was just Oliver and her, hearts entwined, safe within the sanctuary they'd created from the love they shared and the challenges they'd overcome.

The cascading water became a symphony, its crescendo mirroring the rise of their passion. Waves of pleasure surged between them, each tide higher than the last until they crested together in a rush of exultation. It was as if the very essence of Oliver and Lisa melded within this steam-filled chamber, two souls reaching across the boundaries of flesh to intertwine in a moment of pure bliss. Their bodies clung to one another, every curve and contour melding in an intricate puzzle that found its completion only in their embrace.

As the peak of their ardor settled into a gentle ebb, Oliver's arms wrapped around Lisa with a reverence that spoke volumes of his devotion. They stood beneath the warm cascade, hearts still galloping but slowly returning to a tranquil pace. The aftermath of their love was a tangible warmth that saturated the air, mixing with the steam and seeping into their very pores.

Lisa rested her head against Oliver's chest, listening to the steady beat of his heart—a rhythm that had become the most soothing sound in her world. His heartbeat was a reminder of the life they'd built, a thrum of security amidst the undercurrents of danger that always seemed to lurk at the edges of their peaceful existence. Here, shielded by the spray and enfolded in Oliver's embrace, she felt untouchable, bolstered by an intimacy that was both their armor and their reprieve.

Oliver's chin rested atop Lisa's head, his eyes closed

as he breathed in the scent of her hair, the unique fragrance mingled with the steamy humidity. This was their sanctuary, where the roles of protector and protected blurred into a mutual strength. Each droplet of water that washed over them seemed to cleanse away the lurking shadows of their past, renewing their spirits and fortifying their bond.

The connection they shared was not just a physical tie; it was the lifeline that had pulled them through tempests and turmoil. In the afterglow of their union, the sensation of being wholly loved—and loving just as fiercely in return—was an anchor in the chaos of the world outside their shower's embrace.

They held each other, two figures standing strong amidst the mist, their silence speaking louder than words ever could. At this moment, there was no need for declarations or promises; their joined hands, the brush of lips against skin, the shared heat of their bodies—all testified to a love resolute enough to face any challenge that dared to come their way.

Water droplets traced paths along their entwined forms. Oliver's hand cupped Lisa's cheek, his thumb caressing her damp skin as he pulled back just enough to gaze into her eyes. Their breaths mingled, warm and rhythmic, as he pressed his forehead to hers. In this proximity, each whisper was an affirmation, a vow silently strengthening the invisible threads that bound their hearts.

"Every day with you," Oliver murmured, the vibrations of his voice a tactile sensation against her lips, "is a promise renewed."

Lisa's response came not in words but in the tender meeting of their mouths, a kiss that wove through the remnants of steam like a delicate stitch mending any unseen fractures in their lives. Her fingers brushed the nape of Oliver's neck, sending shivers down his spine despite the warmth enfolding them. The simple touch spoke volumes, conveying the depth of her gratitude for the safety and love he provided and for the way he embraced not only her but also her children as his own.

"Here, with you, I find my strength," she whispered back, her hazel eyes reflecting a history of overcoming shadows, now bright with the light of a love that had proven itself unbreakable.

Their promises were not grandiose; they required no audience other than the sanctuary of water and tile that encased them. Each word was a pledge to stand united, to cherish the life they built together brick by brick, to protect their family from the specters of the past that sometimes clawed at the edges of their peace.

The shower's gentle patter underscored their covenant, a soothing rhythm that grounded them in the present—a moment suspended between the thrills and uncertainties of life in their small town. For Oliver, it was a vow to remain vigilant, to be the bulwark against any storm that might arise. For Lisa, each whispered promise was a step further away from the fear that once held her, a declaration of trust in the man who stood before her, and the love that had become her refuge.

Replenished by their shared resolve, they finally turned off the faucet, the cessation of water marking the end of one act and the quiet prelude to the rest of their lives. Stepping out onto the bath mat, their arms remained locked around one another, a mutual anchor as beads of water slipped from their skin and vanished into the fabric beneath their feet.

The air outside the shower embraced them with a cooler touch, but the heat that radiated from their bodies was undiminished—a vestige of their passion and the silent oath that whatever lay beyond the fogged-up bathroom door, they would face it together, as inseparable in spirit as they had been in embrace. Oliver wrapped a towel around Lisa, tucking her close before drying himself off, the air thick with the lingering scent of their union. Their reflections in the fogged-up mirror seemed to smile back at them, a testament to the contentment that enveloped their souls even as the outside world loomed with its challenges and mysteries.

As they made their way to their bedroom, Oliver held Lisa's hand, his touch a steady reassurance that echoed the steadfastness of his love. The soft lamplight cast a warm glow over the room as they settled into bed, their bodies still humming with the echoes of passion shared in the shower. But it wasn't just physical desire that bound them; it was the profound connection forged through trials endured and joys celebrated together.

Wrapped in each other's arms beneath the covers, they lay in comfortable silence, words unnecessary in the cocoon of their togetherness.

Chapter Seventeen

Oliver felt the tension in his shoulders ease as he wrapped his arms around his parents. The air was sharp with the scent of pine and wood smoke, the crackle of the bonfires blending with the murmur of voices from the town square.

"Thank you," his father whispered, his voice rough with unshed tears. "For all you have done. Now, we can finally close this chapter. And we have gained another grandson. We're going to see little Sammy next week."

His mother, always the stoic one, trembled slightly within the circle of their embrace, her walls crumbling after years of self-imposed isolation. Oliver could feel the heartbeat of his family syncing at that moment, the pulse of forgiveness threading through them all, promising a future where the pain of the past would no longer shadow their every step.

"It's time to heal," Lisa said, her eyes glistening with

the reflection of the flames and the depth of her conviction.

They stepped back, hands still clasped, forming an unbroken chain. Oliver knew it wouldn't be easy—the road to reconciliation was wrought with the unknown—but the warmth in his chest burgeoned at the thought of mending the fragmented bonds. At least all the unanswered questions were gone. The only one left still lingering in his parents' minds was why Michelle hadn't come to them before leaving town. But that was one they'd never get the answer to. And one they'd have to let go of over time.

The thrum of excitement drew them toward the heart of the small town. The square was aglow with strings of lights intertwined with the boughs of spruce trees, casting an ethereal glow over the gathering. Laughter danced on the wind, harmonizing with the strains of a fiddle and the rhythmic stomp of boots on the wooden stage.

"Look at this," Lisa murmured, her voice tinged with wonder as they approached the celebration.

Tables laden with potluck dishes lined the perimeter. Freshly baked salmon, hearty stews, and berry pies competed for attention, their aromas mingling with the crisp night air. Children weaved between adults, their giggles punctuating the music, while elderly couples swayed gently, the lines of time softened in the amber light and the promise of spring around the corner.

"Never thought I'd see the day when I would be able to stop wondering what happened to Michelle and just move on," Oliver's father said, his tone laced with awe as he took in the sight of the town united, the undercurrent of suspense replaced by the thrill of community spirit.

"Neither did I," Oliver agreed, but there was hope in his voice now, an enthusiasm for life that had been absent for too long.

As they joined the festivities, the townspeople welcomed them with open arms and shared stories, each anecdote a stitch in the fabric of their collective history. They were characters in a larger narrative, one of resilience and the enduring power of the human spirit. Each handshake, each hug, each knowing nod spoke volumes, acknowledging the shared trials and tribulations that had brought them to this point of jubilation.

"Here's to new beginnings," Lisa toasted, raising a cup of apple cider.

"New beginnings," echoed the crowd, their voices rising to the heavens, a chorus of determination and unity.

Oliver looked around at the faces illuminated by the flickering light, his children's bright eyes, Lisa's radiant smile, and his parents, now part of the fold once more. The chill of the night was kept at bay by the warmth of their togetherness, the promise of tomorrow fueling the pulsing heart of the small town.

Amid the revelry, he knew this was more than a celebration—it was a declaration of their collective strength, a testament to the enduring nature of love and the indomitable spirit of a community reborn. Oliver Thompson, surrounded by his family and friends, felt a profound sense of peace settle within him as the thrilling chapter of uncertainty closed and the next began—one filled with the anticipation of healing and the sweet taste of redemption.

The flicker of lanterns danced across Lisa's face as she pulled Oliver aside, her eyes locking with his in a way that told him this was a moment to be engraved in the story of their hearts. The din of the ongoing celebration —a symphony of laughter and clinking glasses—faded into a distant hum as she reached for both his hands, pressing them gently against her belly.

"Oliver," she whispered, her voice barely rising above the whisper of the wind, "we're going to have another baby."

His breath hitched, the world tilting on its axis as the weight of her words sank in. A rush of emotions overtook him—surprise, elation, a fierce protectiveness—and he swept her into an embrace that spoke volumes of the love and hope that surged like a tide within him. Their children, Ethan, Abigail, Julia, and Daniel, gathered around, their expressions blooming from curiosity to wonder as they grasped the magnitude of the revelation.

"Really? You don't think you have enough?" Ethan's voice cracked, his teenage bravado giving way to child-like awe, while Abigail's squeal of delight cut through the night air. "Yay, another baby!"

Julia clung to her mother's leg, beaming up at her, and even young Daniel's eyes sparkled with a sense of understanding as he shuffled closer.

"Really," Lisa confirmed, her smile infectious, a secret shared now igniting joy amongst them. The family huddled together, a fortress of warmth against the cool Alaskan night, their laughter mingling with the crackle of bonfires.

At the edge of the circle of light, Oliver's parents watched, the lines of past sorrows softening in the glow of their grandchildren's happiness. They stepped forward, a tentative movement that bridged the distance of years and heartaches. His father cleared his throat, a simple gesture that nonetheless captured everyone's attention.

"Lisa, Oliver," he began, his voice thick with emotion, "your courage and love have been a beacon for all of us. To see our family grow, it's... it's more than we could have hoped for."

His mother nodded, her eyes shimmering with unshed tears as she added, "We are here for you, for all of you, to support and cherish this new life. And, of course, babysit whenever needed."

Their words, laden with sincerity and remorse for years lost, wrapped around the Thompson family like a gentle wave, washing away the remnants of old wounds. The future, once a canvas stained by the shadows of the past, now glistened with the promise of new beginnings.

As the stars blinked above and the town rejoiced, the Thompsons stood united, their hearts beating in rhythm with the quiet thrill of anticipation. For in that hushed moment of suspense and tenderness, they celebrated not just the survival of their love but its blossoming under the most unexpected of circumstances—a testament to the resilience that thrived in the depths of the Alaskan wilds.

Forever and always.

The End

Cover design by Juan Villar Padron,
https://www.juanjpadron.com

Special thanks to my editor Janell Parque
http://janellparque.blogspot.com/

Contents